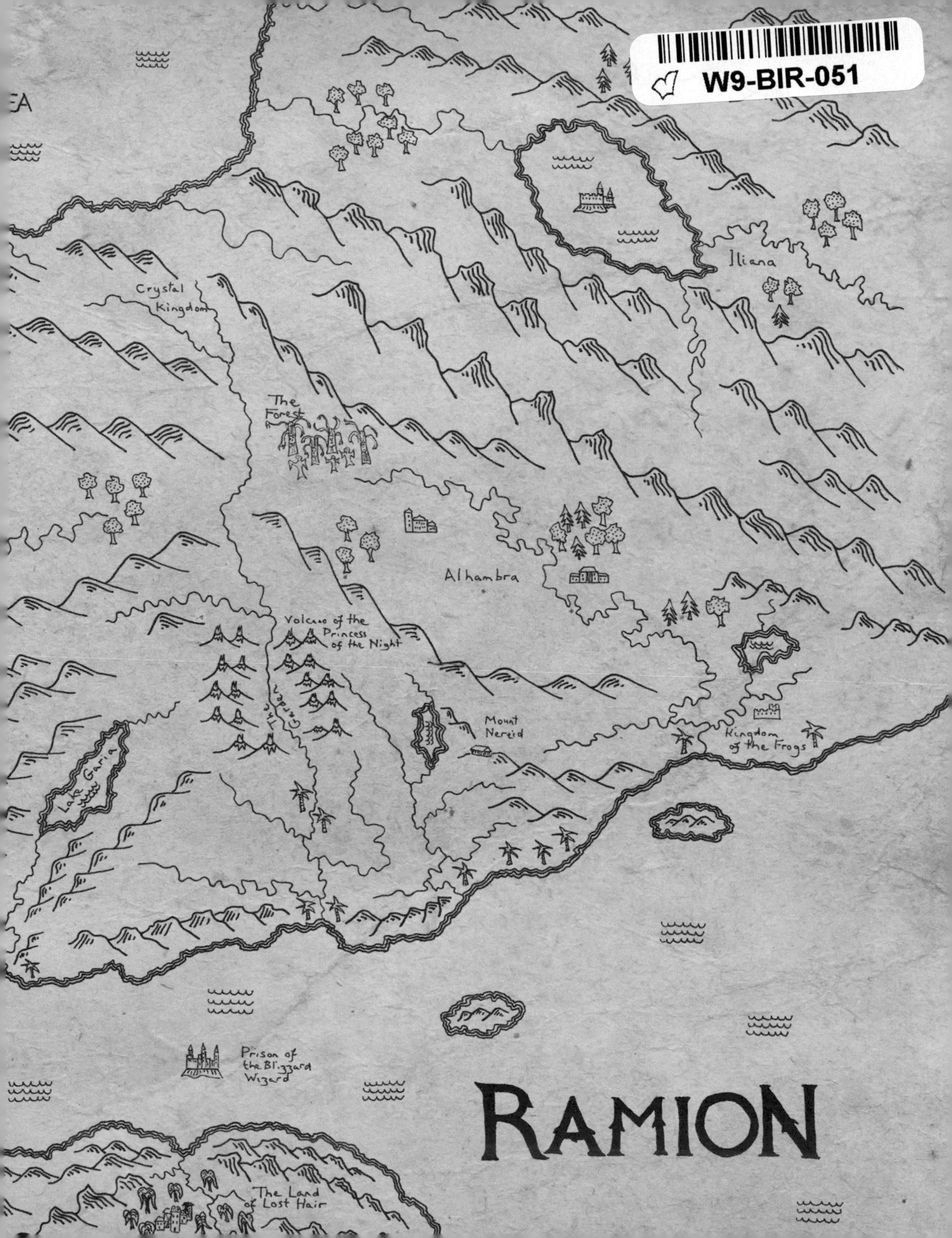
Crystal Kingdom
Iliana
The Forest
Alhambra
Volcano of the Princess of the Night
The Garden
Mount Nereid
Kingdom of the Frogs
Lake Garia
Prison of the Blizzard Wizard
The Land of Lost Hair
RAMION

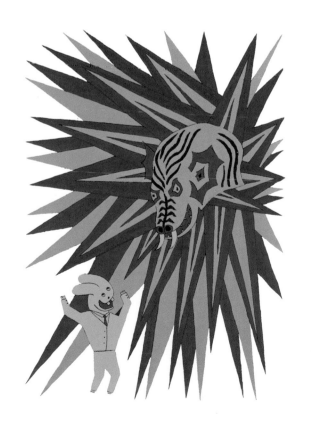

THE CRYSTAL KEY

Published by

Perronet Press

www.ramion-books.com

Copyright © Text and illustrations

Frank Hinks 2019

A CIP record for this book is available from the British Library

ISBN: 9781909938137

Printed in China by CP Printing Ltd.
Layout by Jennifer Stephens
Font designer - Bajo La Luna Producciones

TALES OF RAMION
THE
CRYSTAL KEY

FRANK HINKS

Perronet
2019

TALES OF RAMION

THE GARDENER

Lord of Ramion, guardian and protector

THE GUIDE

Friend and servant of the Gardener

SNUGGLE

Dream Lord sent to protect the boys from the witch Griselda

ERIC AND DRAGO

Friendly dragons, but Drago has the dreadful habit of spitting

JULIUS
ALEXANDER
BENJAMIN

Three brothers who long for adventure

SCROOEY-LOOEY

*Greedy, rude, half-mad rabbit,
a friend of the boys*

THE LION OF ICING

*Melts in the rain, in sunshine
springs to life again*

GRISELDA THE GRUNCH

A witch who longs to eat the boys

THE DIM DAFT DWARVES

Julioso, Aliano, Benjio, Griselda's guards

BORIS

Griselda's pet skull, strangely fond of her

ALBEE THE ALBATROSS

Spy of the Princess, harbingder of doom

RAVENOUS

Great, green, scaly monster, only eats boys called Benjamin

PRINCESS OF THE NIGHT

Lord of Nothingness, source of evil

GNARGS

Warrior servants of the Princess

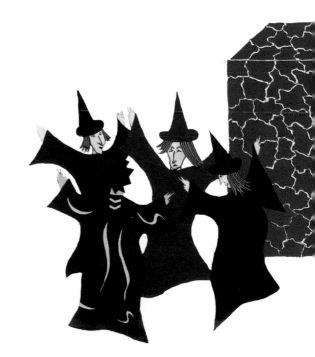

Chapter One

L**ate one afternoon a van arrived in the village driven by a horrid hag. On the outside were painted the words "Mrs G.'s Best Balloons" and pictures of the most beautiful balloons in the world. The van stopped outside The Old Vicarage and Julius, Alexander and Benjamin ran up to it.

"Ah my dear little boys," said Mrs G. rubbing her hands with glee and thinking of her supper. "You look so good for eat … I mean what balloons would you like to buy? For you a special price – 1p."

"Red!" "Blue!" "Green!" the boys replied, handing over the money to Mrs G. who, with a toot, toot, toot, drove away fast.

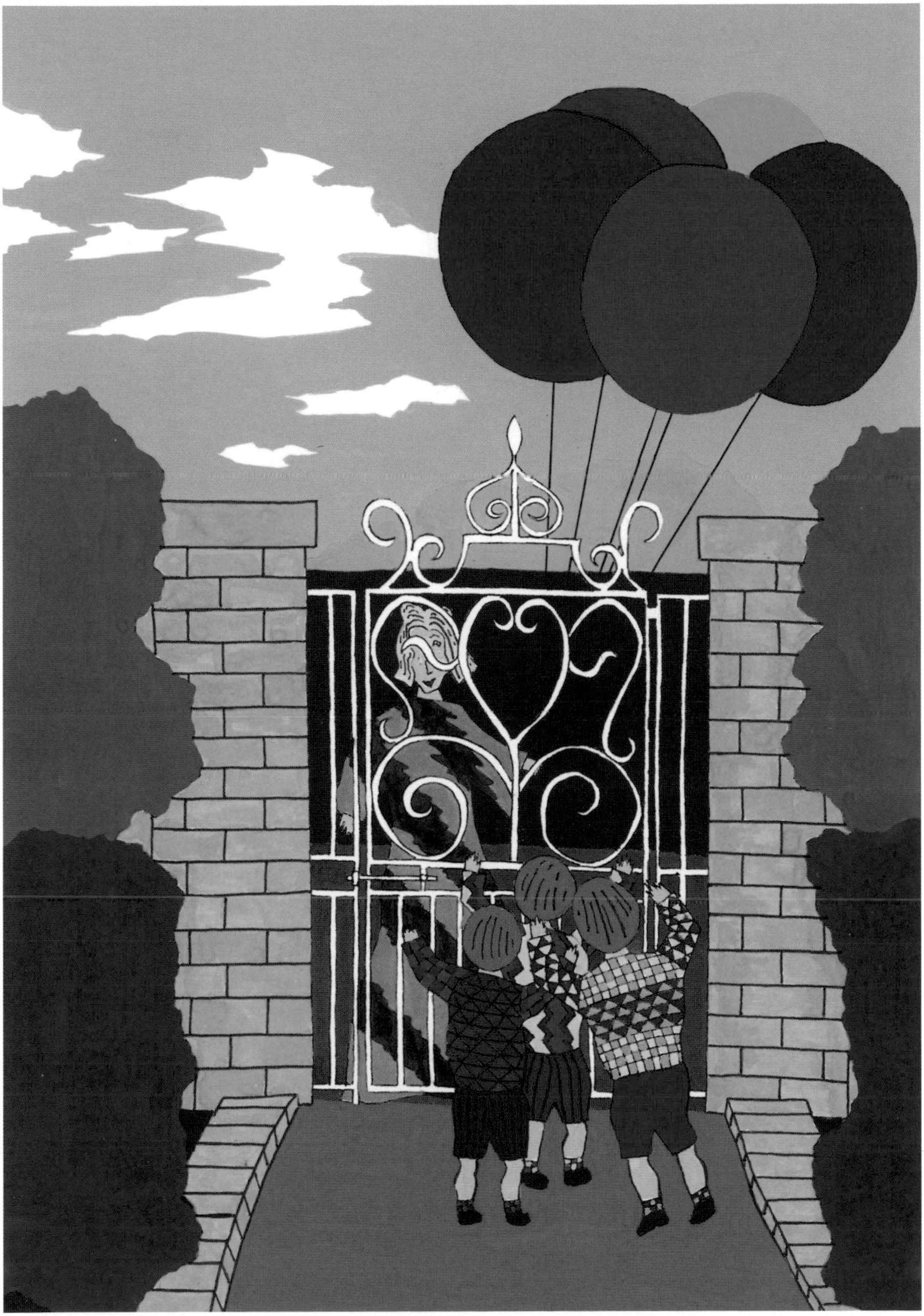

The boys ran back into the garden holding their balloons by the string. Suddenly the string wrapped itself tight around their wrists, the balloons got bigger and bigger and the boys floated up into the air.

The boys' screams awoke Snuggle. The cat jumped out of his basket, and ran into the garden, as the boys rose above the trees, and a strange wind blew and carried them away, towards a ruined tower in a glade deep within the forest.

"Don't worry!" Snuggle shouted. "I shall rescue you."

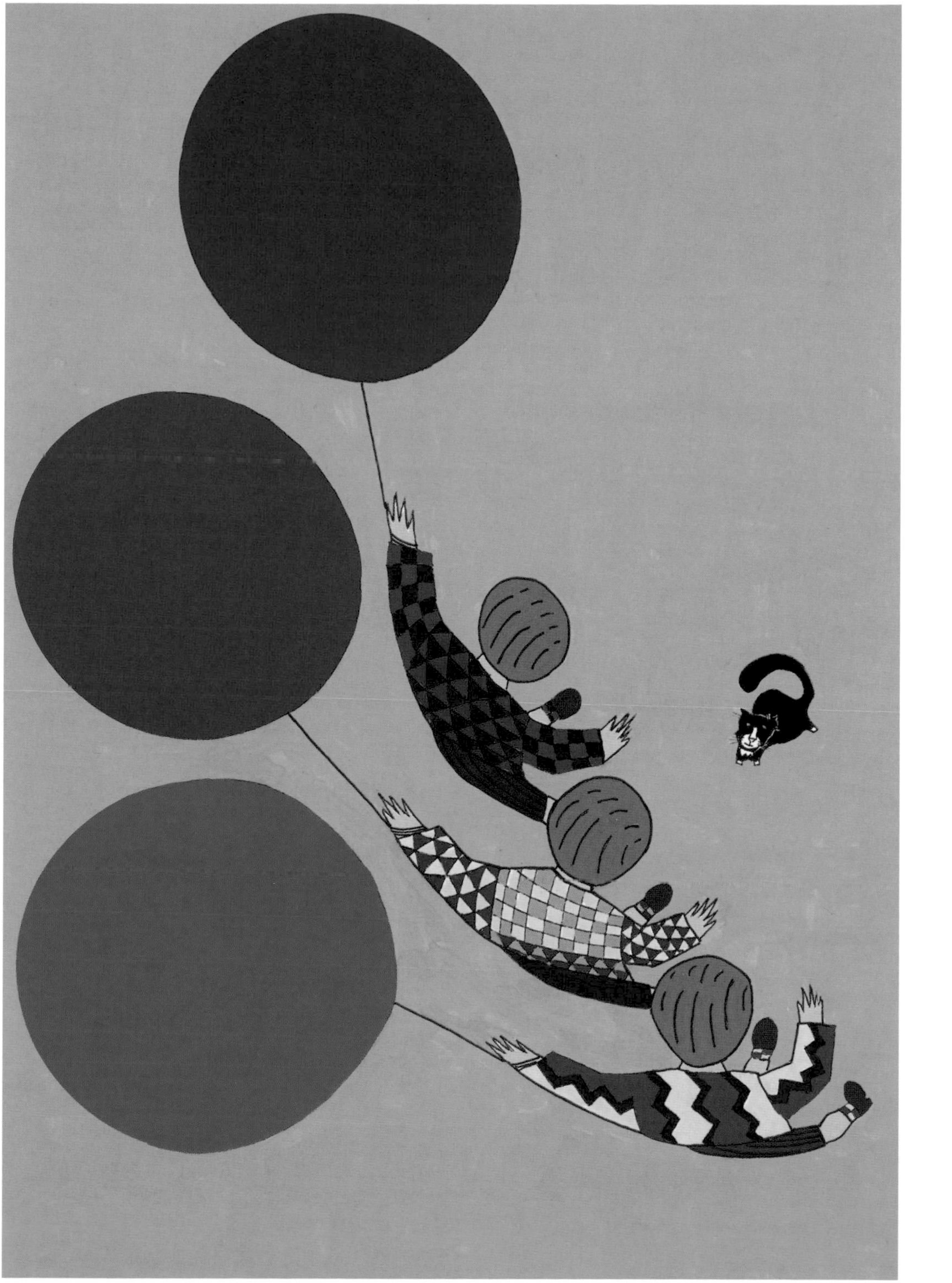

As Mrs G. drove into the glade, she changed into the witch Griselda. She called out to her guards: "Is the fattening mixture ready?"

Boris the skull was floating above the tower, looking towards the village. He hurried to Griselda and hissed: "They come! They come! I can see three balloons: one red, one blue, one green."

"And underneath – my supper!" murmured Griselda licking her lips.

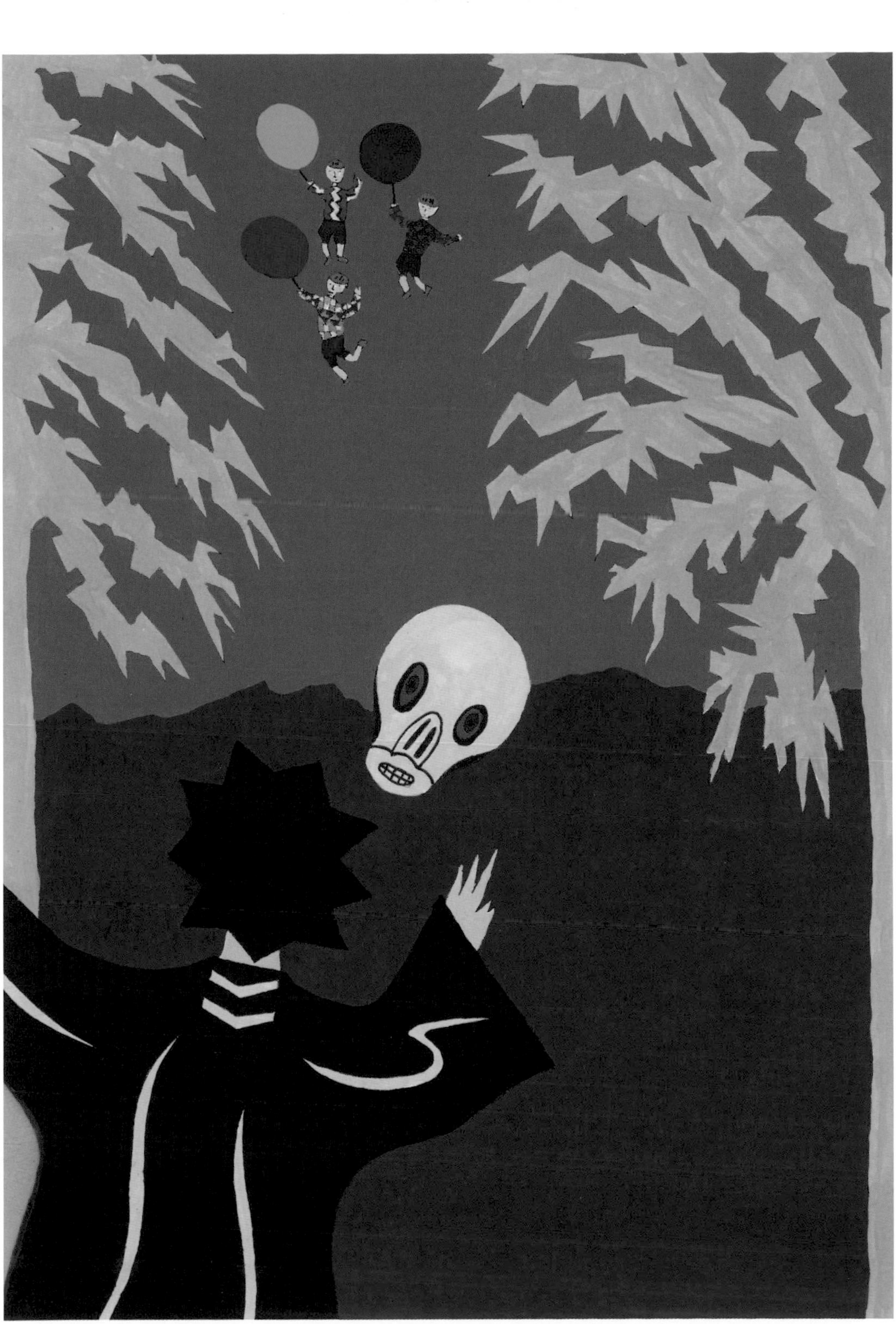

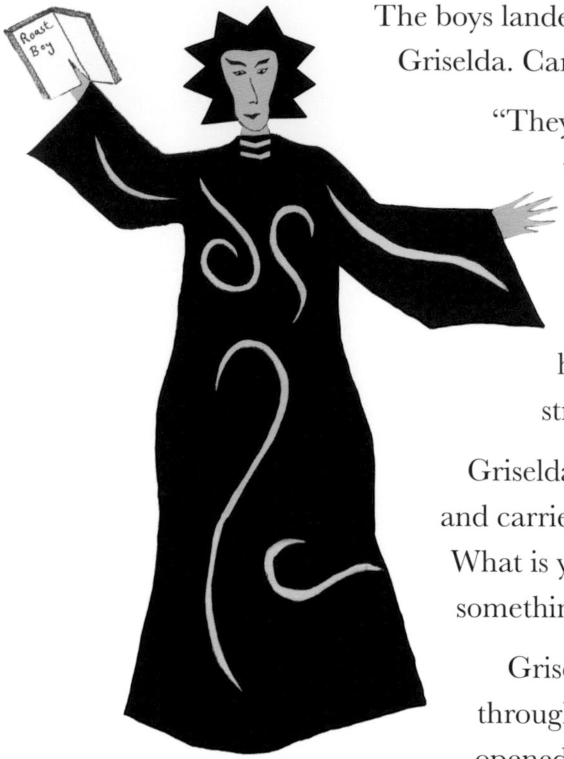
Roast
Boy

The boys landed with a bump just in front of Griselda. Carefully she surveyed them.

"They need fattening up. Guards! Put them in the cages."

The dwarves, Julioso, Aliano and Benjio, ran to catch the boys, who stood back to back, and fought hard. But the dwarves were too strong, and threw them in the cages.

Griselda took a bowl of fattening mixture and carried it to a cage. "My dear little ... What is your name? Ah yes. Benjamin. Have something to eat."

Griselda pushed a wooden spoon through the bars of Benjamin's cage. He opened his mouth, and with a cry spat the mixture in Griselda's eye. "You will pay for that, you little scum. Guards! I want them fed."

The dwarves entered the cages, and though each boy put up a fight, it was not long before they were fed.

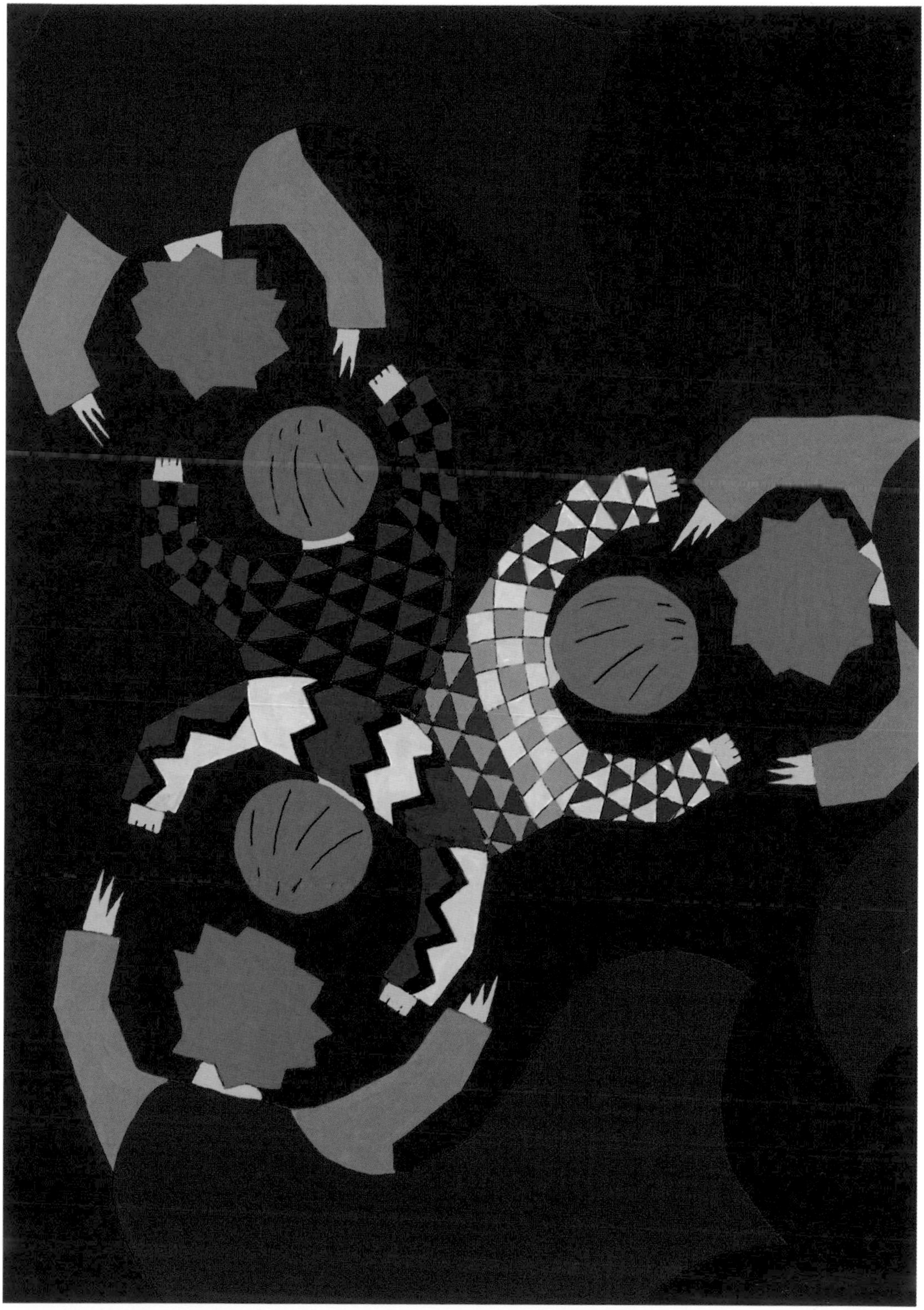

Griselda picked up a cookery book.

"Now, let me see. Roast dragon. No, not that: dragons are much too tough and stringy. Roast unicorn: nice, but very hard to get. Ah, here it is. Boys. With roast Julius I shall have a sauce of dragon's blood and mashed newt. Stewed Alexander will be delicious with sewer water, diced maggots and wings of bat, and with Benjamin on toast, wriggling worms will be best.

The witch turned to her guards. "Go and get the ingredients," she ordered. "Quick! Quick! Hurry! Hurry! I am feeling hungry." She licked her lips and rubbed her belly.

With moans and groans the dwarves ran off to buy the ingredients from the shop.

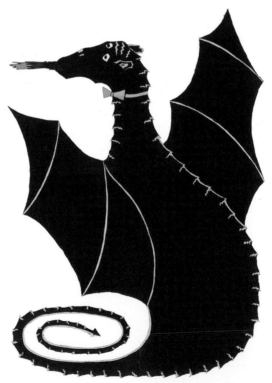

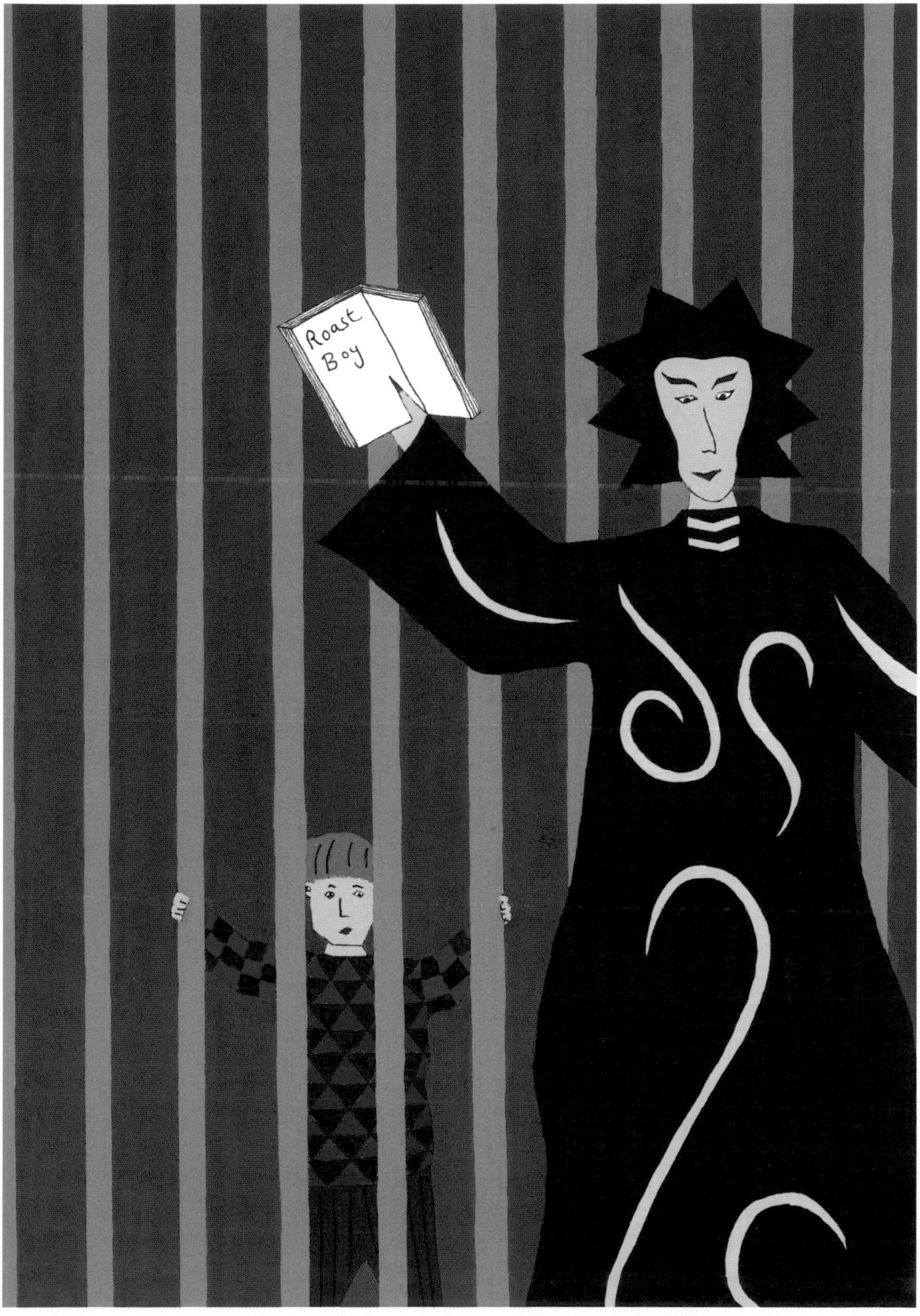
Roast Boy

CHAPTER TWO

When Snuggle saw the boys float off, he jumped up on to the garden wall, down the other side, over the road, across the field, always looking in the sky at the balloons of red, blue and green, and the boys dangling underneath, disappearing fast into the distance.

"Do not worry: I shall save you," Snuggle murmured as his mind reached out to the boys.

"Snuggle is on the way," whispered Julius to his brothers. "I heard him in my mind."

"So did I."

"And I."

"Let's try to reply."

Their minds reached out to Snuggle.

"We have been captured by Griselda."

"She has fattened us up."

"She is going to eat us for her supper."

"I'm running fast. Delay her as much as you can."

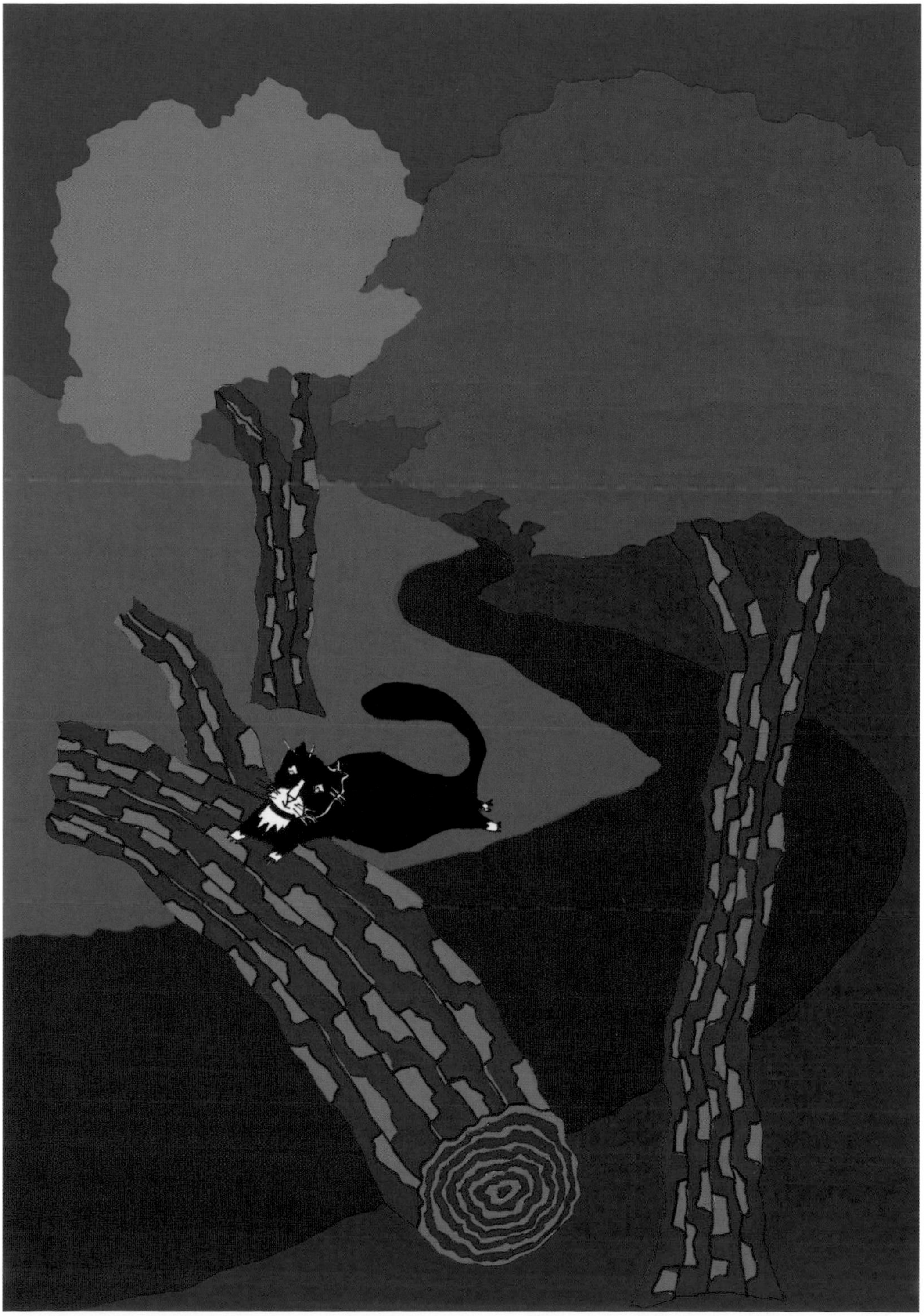

The three boys thought hard. Alexander was a treasure hunter, a great collector of sticks and stones. He looked through his pockets, found a piece of wood in the shape of a Y and whispered to his brothers: "I could take the elastic from Benjamin's trousers, make a catapult, and get the guards to spill the ingredients for supper."

Benjamin was not keen, but in the end agreed. When the guards returned laden with the ingredients, Alexander took the catapult from his pocket, picked up a stone and fired at a wasp's nest in a tree just above the guards. The wasps rose up in a swarm and swooping down attacked them.

"Ow!" cried the dwarf Julioso, as he tried to brush the wasps away, and dropped the dragon's blood and mashed newt over Aliano.

"Ugh!" cried Aliano, as dragon's blood ran down his neck, and he poured sewer water and maggots over Benjio.

"Pong!" cried Benjio, as the sewer water ran down his neck, and he dropped the wings of bat and wriggling worms over Julioso.

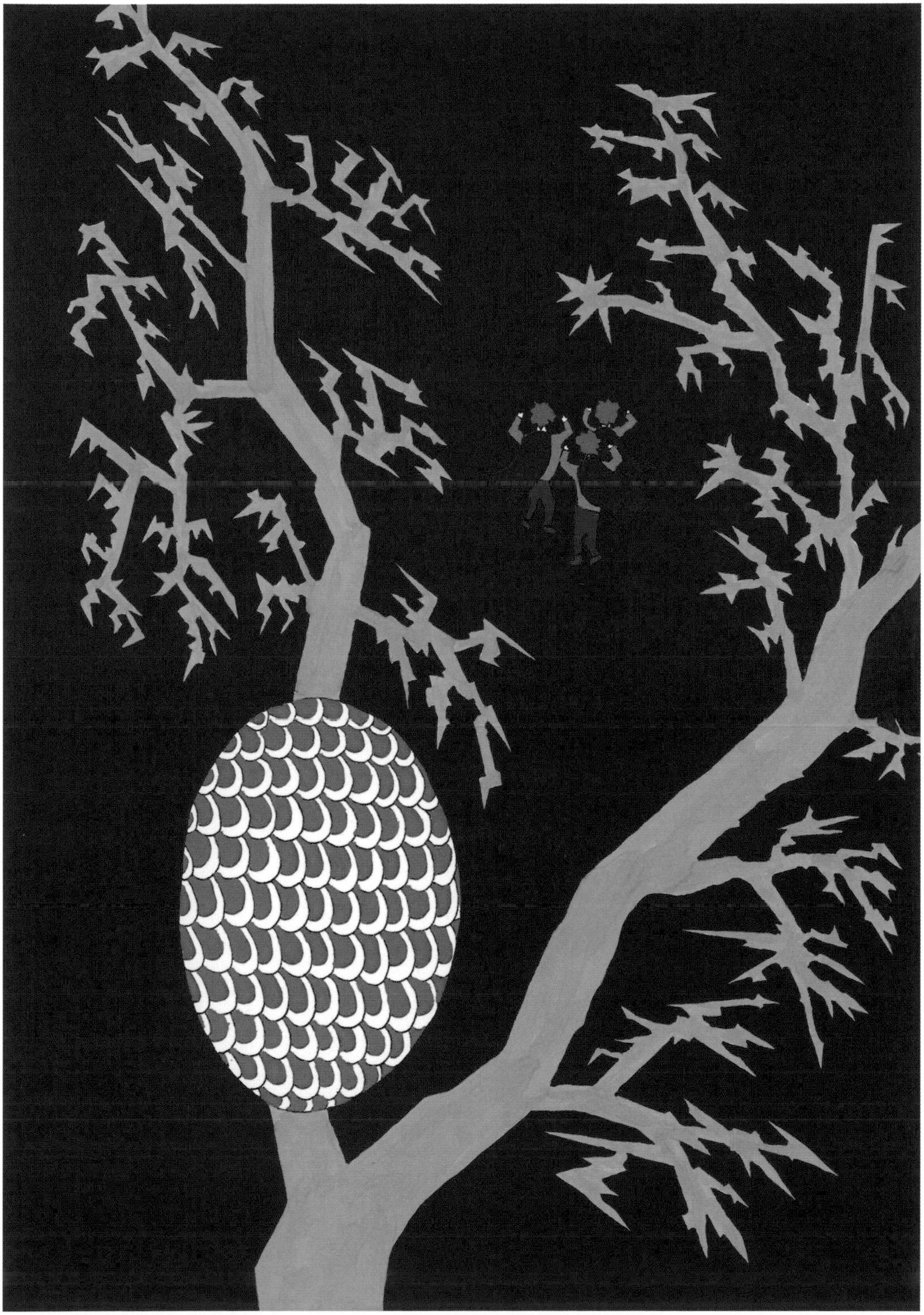

Griselda heard the noise and ran out of the tower. "Guards! Guards! What is the matter? Where are the ingredients?" The guards pointed to the ground. "I'm not eating them. Get some more." The guards were tired and did not move. "Get out of here! Before I reduce your height to two foot three."

The guards were sensitive about their lack of height. They felt that they were already small enough. So with moans and groans the guards stumbled off. By the time they returned it was nearly dark.

"Here they come," whispered Alexander.

"Out with the catapult," hissed Julius.

"No. Put it away. Keep very quiet," purred Snuggle, who had had a few adventures on the way, and had only just arrived.

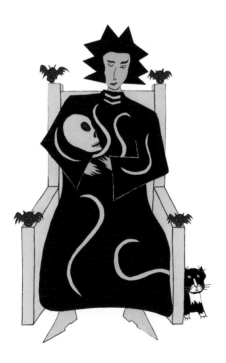

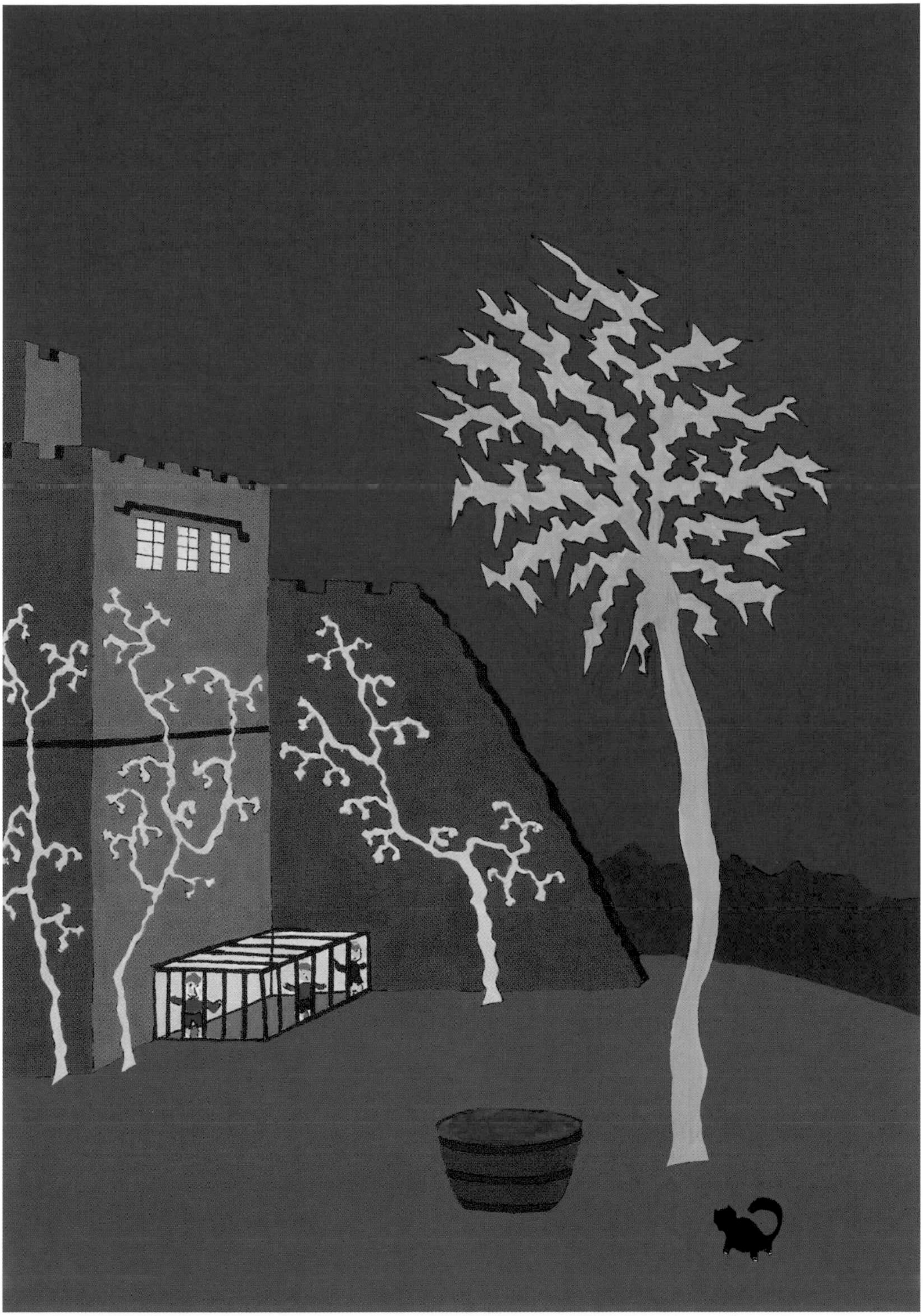

The dwarves went into the tower, followed silently by Snuggle.

"Start preparing the food," ordered Griselda, licking her lips, and suddenly feeling in a more cheerful mood. "Boris! Come here. I shall scratch your bony head."

"Mistress! Yes!" hissed Boris excitedly, his eye sockets beginning to spin, as he floated to Griselda and rested on her knee. She cradled him in her arms, and scratched and tickled his bony head. His eye sockets flashed in ecstasy.

Snuggle raised a paw, and took the key to the fattening cages out of the witch's pocket. Griselda looked round and screamed, "Boris! Stop that cat!" Boris floated off and hid. "Guards! Get that cat!"

The dwarves ran after Snuggle, but not fast, for his claws were very sharp. Snuggle threw the key to Julius, and disappeared into the dark.

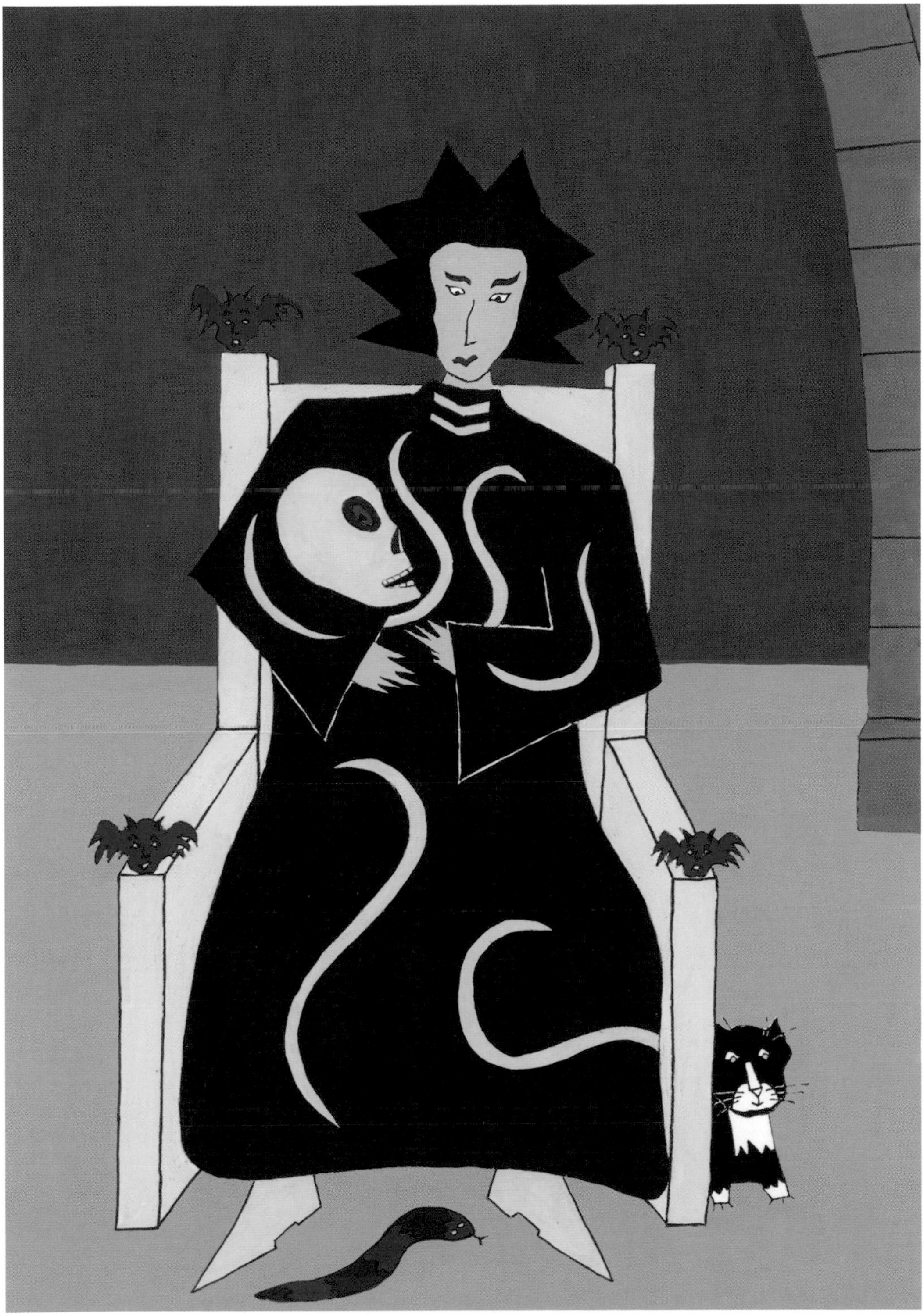

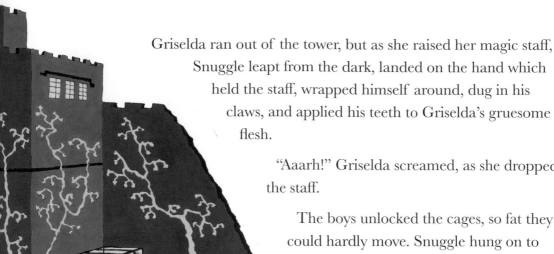

Griselda ran out of the tower, but as she raised her magic staff, Snuggle leapt from the dark, landed on the hand which held the staff, wrapped himself around, dug in his claws, and applied his teeth to Griselda's gruesome flesh.

"Aaarh!" Griselda screamed, as she dropped the staff.

The boys unlocked the cages, so fat they could hardly move. Snuggle hung on to Griselda's hand, burying claws and teeth more deeply, as she tried to pick up her magic staff, and stepping backwards, tripped over Benjamin, who was bending over (his trousers without any elastic had fallen down around his ankles). She fell into the magic cauldron, and with a scream and loud meow, she and Snuggle disappeared. As Griselda vanished, her magic was destroyed, and the boys became their normal size.

"Snuggle! Snuggle! I'm coming after you," Benjamin cried, as he too jumped into the magic cauldron. With a yell, he disappeared.

Julius and Alexander stretched out their hands, held each other tight, and crying, "Benje! We're coming after you," followed him into the cauldron, and also disappeared.

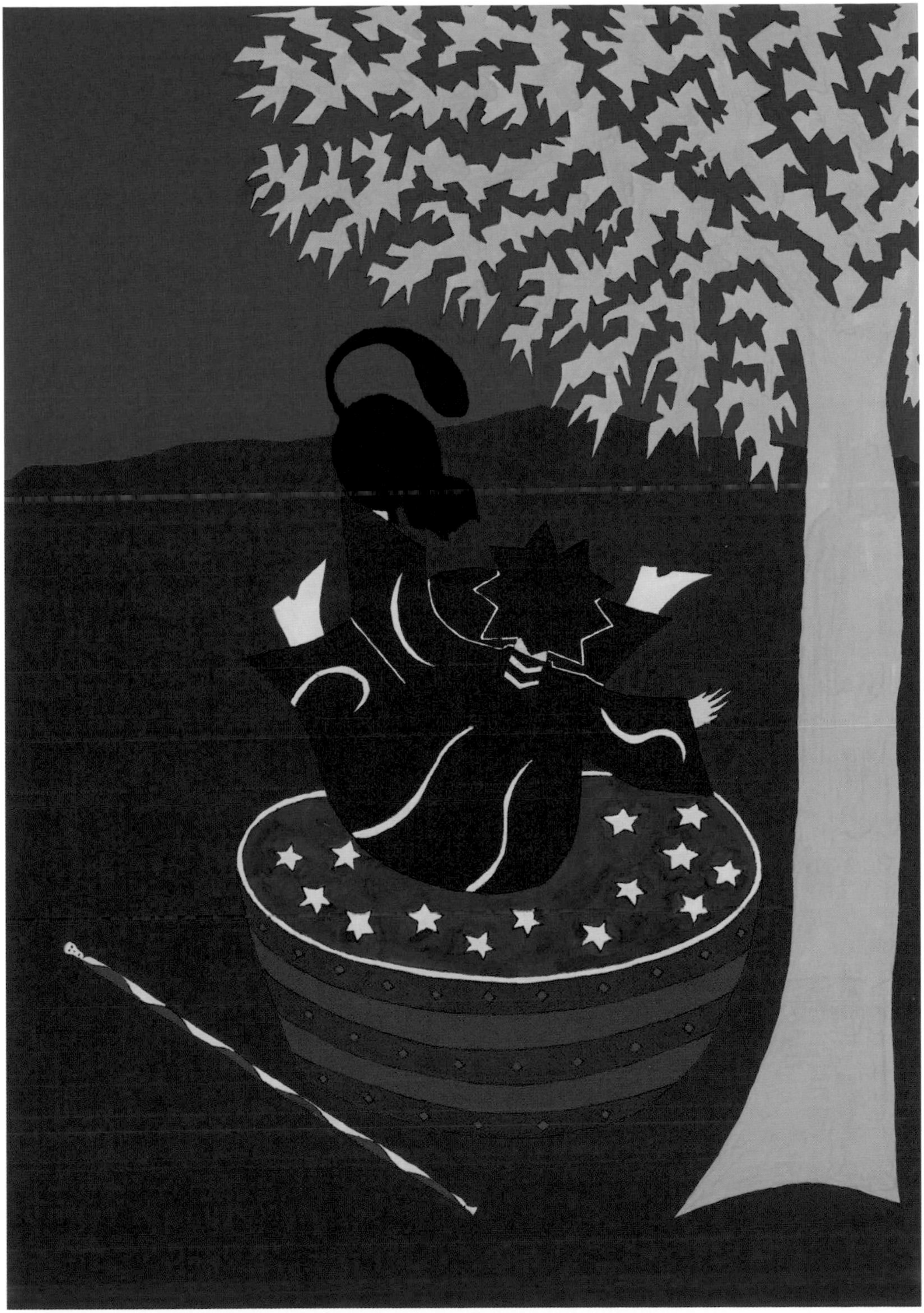

Chapter Three

Benjamin fell and fell through the void, until he landed in a cold, dark cave. Carefully he felt along the walls, trying to hold his trousers up. As they slipped down around his ankles, he tripped over a stick, tumbled down and began to cry. But then he rolled over and picked up the stick, swished it through the air, and feeling more brave started to stab at the vast, dark shadows in the cave.

The shadows seemed to move, and when he gave the largest one a prod, it grunted, rose to its feet and breathed out fire. It was a dragon.

"Do not cook me!" screamed Benjamin in alarm.

But the dragon was only lighting torches on the walls around the cave. With one eye he looked at the little boy, then smiled. "Hello, Benje."

"Hello, Eric," replied Benjamin, recognising the dragon, relieved that they had met before.

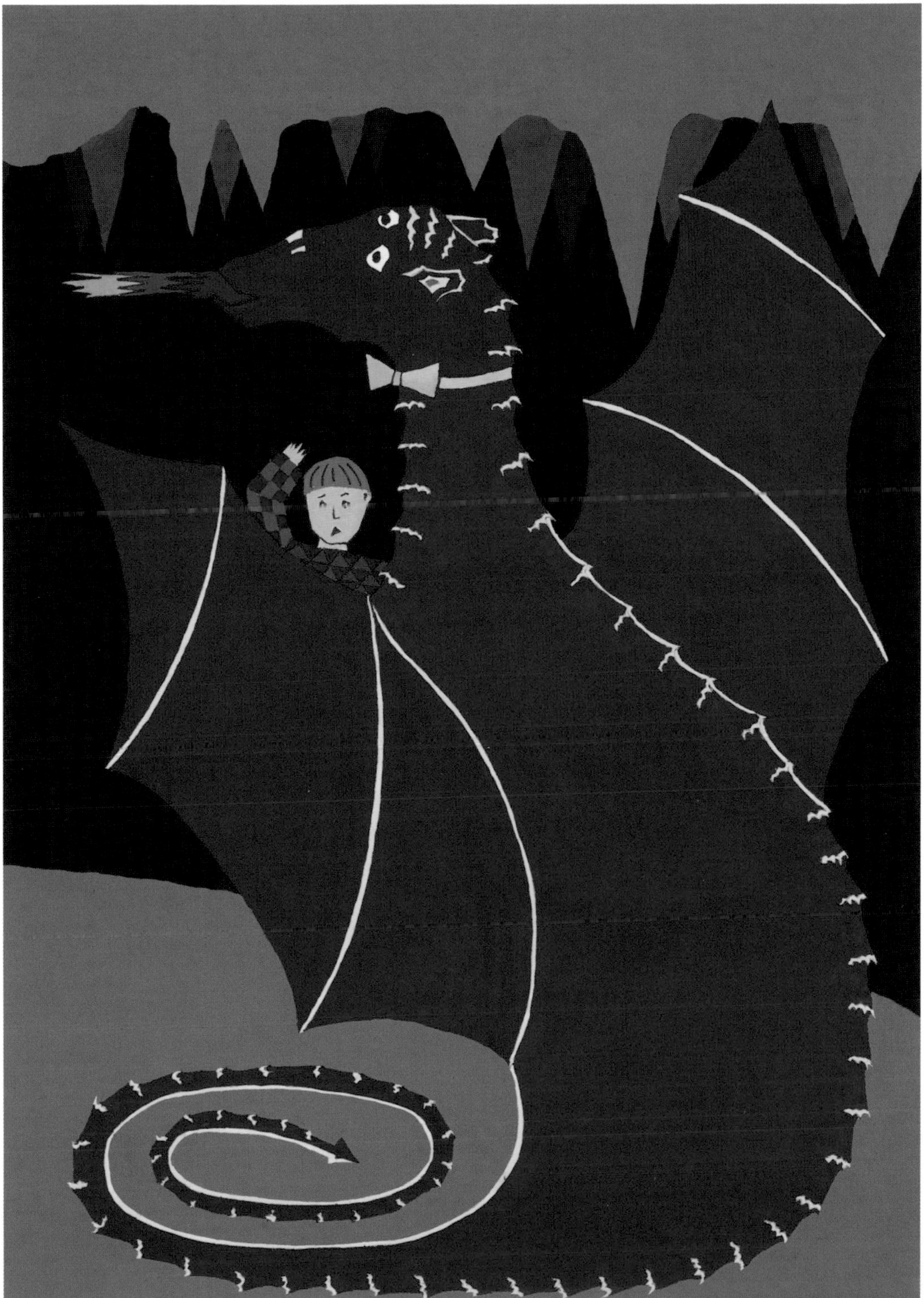

"You tickled me with your stick. Come and have some tea." Eric led the way through the cavern. At the far end a shadow stirred. "Maud, my dear, we have a guest for tea. Come and meet Benje."

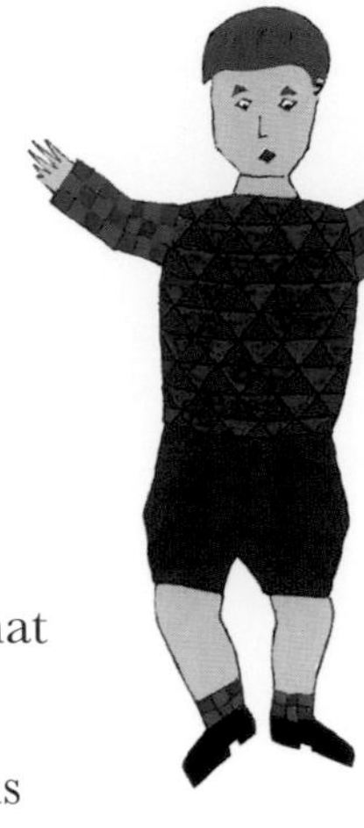

"What is a benje?" yawned Maud sleepily.

"A little boy," said Benjamin. "Benje is my name. Where is your son Drago?"

"Drago is outside. He is in disgrace," said Eric gruffly. "What for? For spitting. There are few habits in a dragon worse than spitting. On Christmas Day Drago spat and all our decorations went up in flames. Then last week he spat and burnt a hole in Maud's best tablecloth. Drago is forever breathing fire in the wrong place."

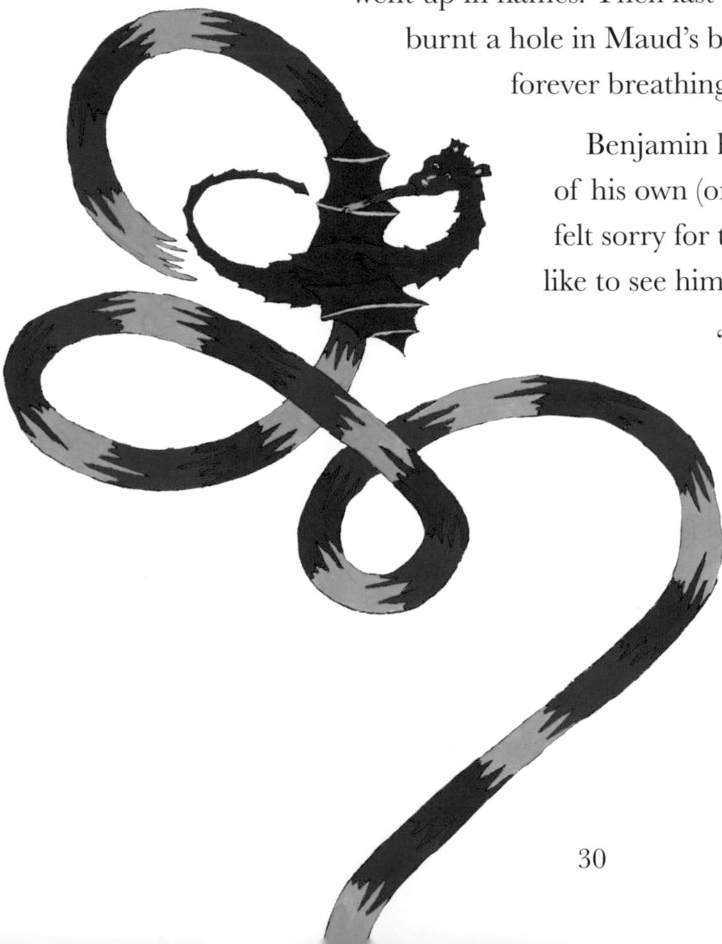

Benjamin had some disgusting habits of his own (or so his parents said). He felt sorry for the little dragon. "I would like to see him. Can we go outside?"

"After a cup of tea."

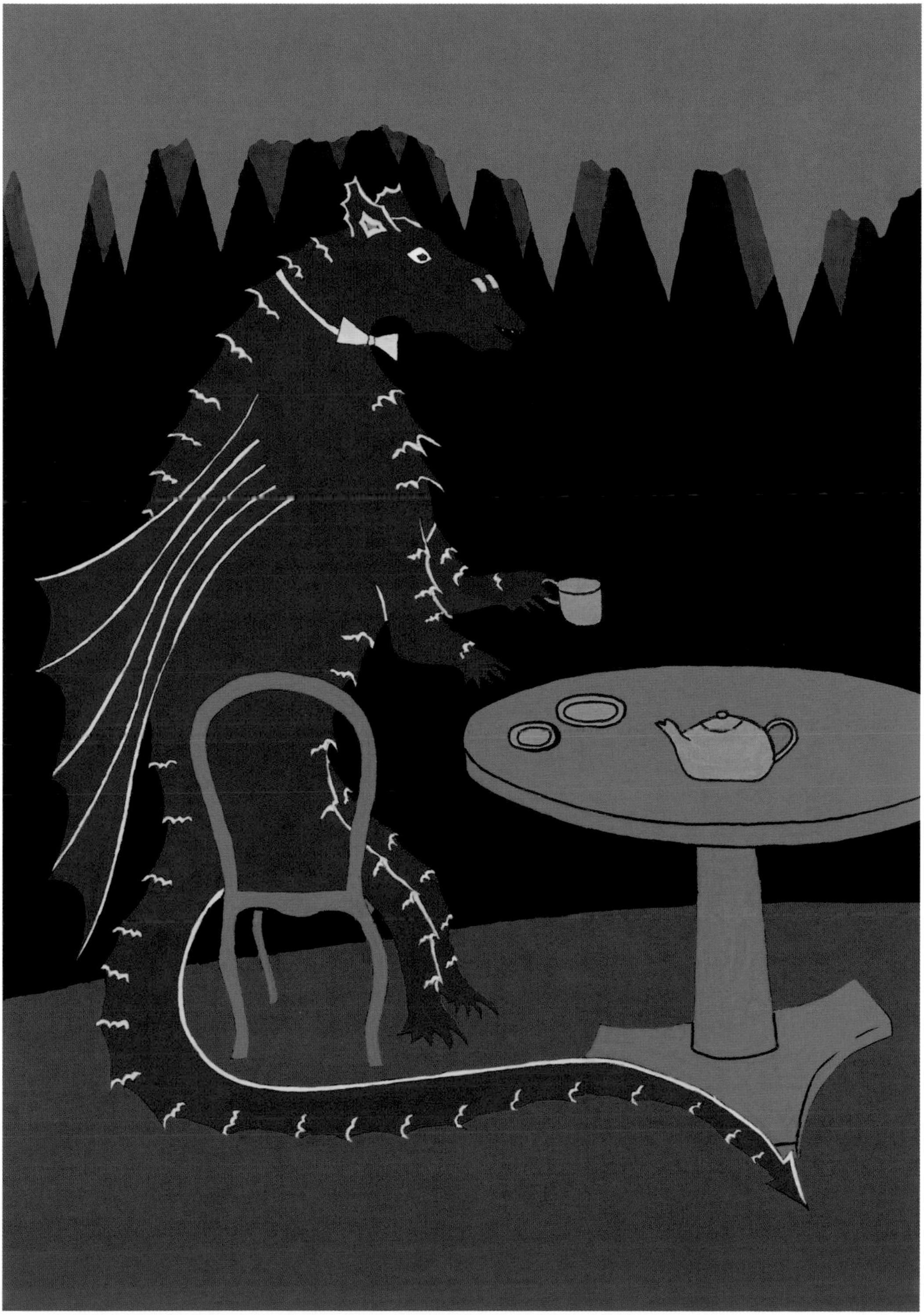

Maud put elastic in Benjamin's trousers. Then the boy got on to Eric's back and was carried out of the cavern and put down beside a lake.

When Drago saw Benjamin he rose into the air, and showing off, looped-the-loop, flew upside down with tail curled round, and spat out a ball of flame: it hit his tail.

"Ow!" roared Drago landing beside the lake, and dipping his tail into the water: there was a hiss and cloud of steam.

"What brings you here?" asked Drago.

Benjamin told the dragons what had happened.

"Griselda is no friend of dragons," said Eric. "She is always wanting our blood for spells and sauces. We'll take you to the Garden. The Gardener will know what to do."

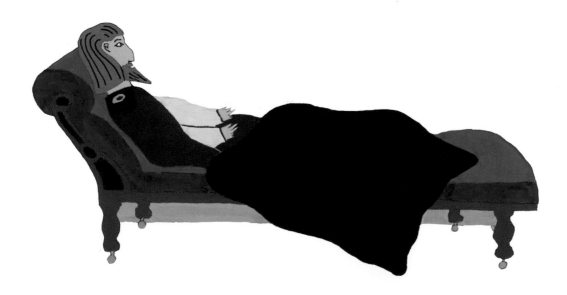

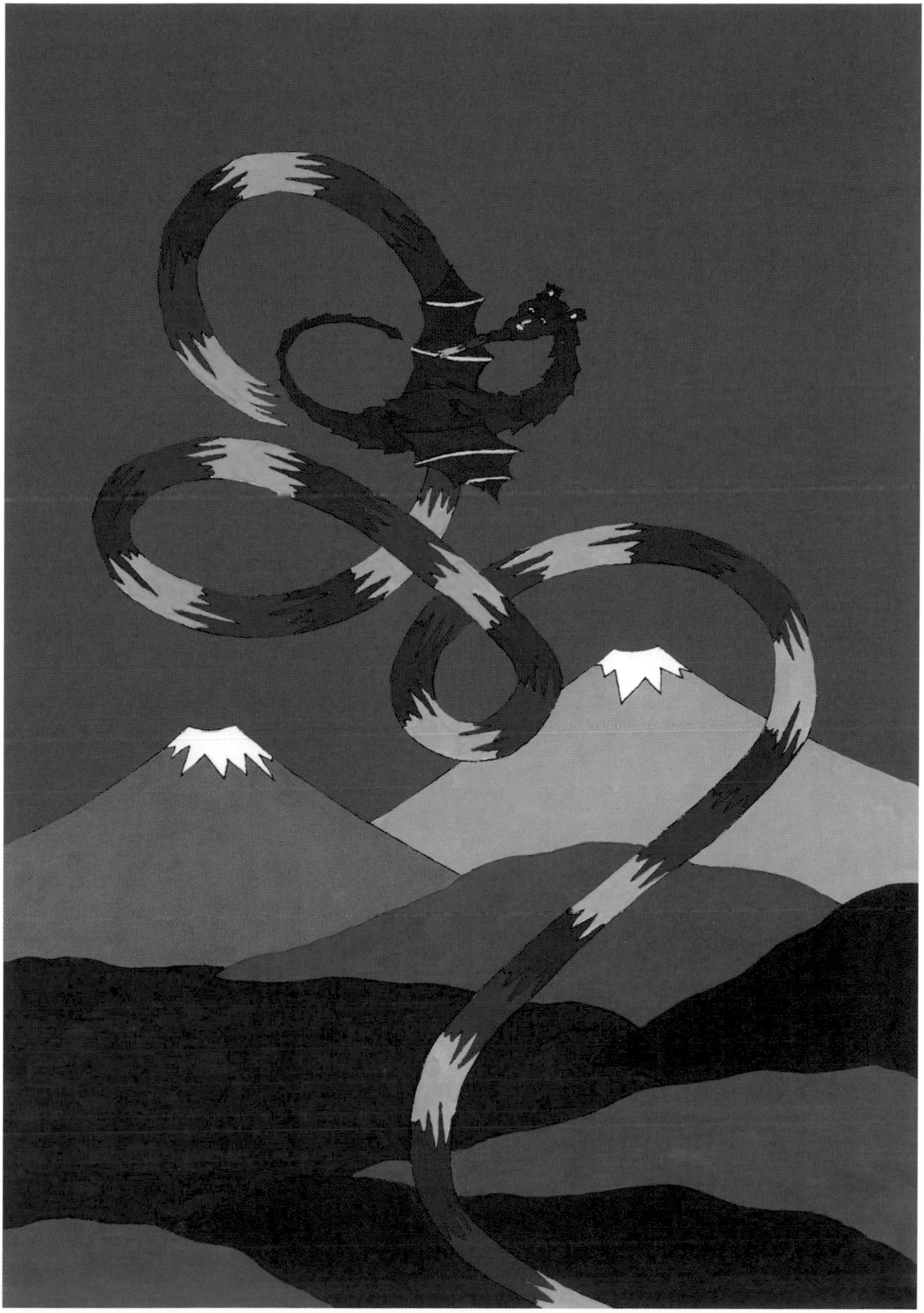

CHAPTER FOUR

Julius and Alexander fell and fell through the void. They strained to see, but all was blackness. They landed on a barren hillside, and looked around at distant hills, jagged peaks of rock, stunted windswept trees.

"We need brave thoughts," said Julius.

"Knights in armour," suggested Alexander.

"Knights in armour slaying dragons, and rescuing damsels in a dress."

"Why in a dress?"

"I don't know. In story books they always say that they are in a dress."

At that moment up rode a knight, clothed in white, sword by side, lance in hand, leading two ponies by the reins.

"Young sirs," he cried, "why are you alone in this barren land?"

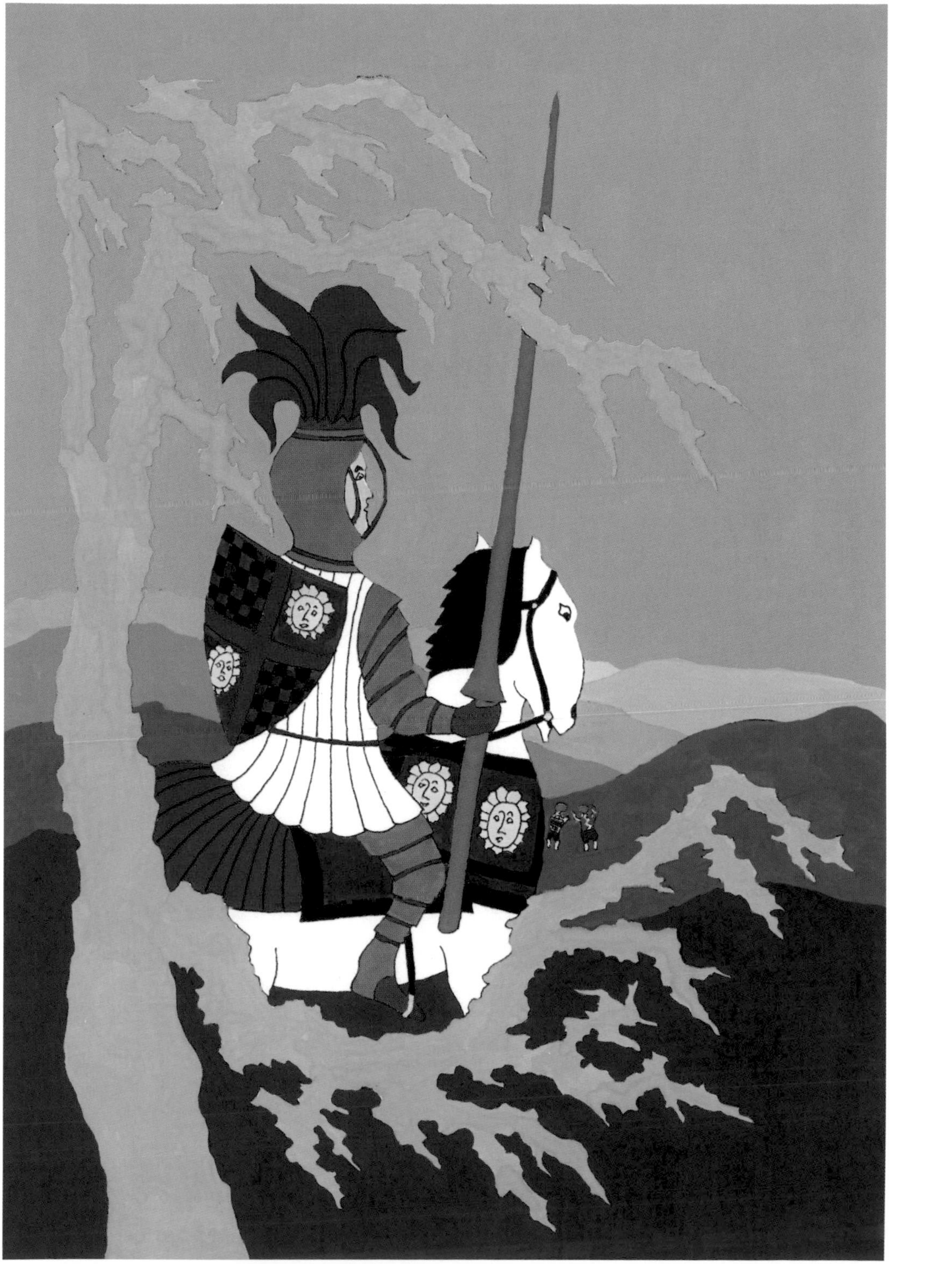

"We are looking for our brother."

"And our cat."

"I know nothing of a cat. Damsels in distress are more my line, but if you wish you may ride with me, be my squires, cook my tea. Come mount the ponies. We must ride."

The boys scrambled on the ponies' backs and rode after their new Lord and Master. The knight told them of fights and noble deeds, dragons slain and damsels rescued, how he was the greatest knight in the Kingdom. Then a mouse ran in front of the knight, his horse reared up and the knight fell off, lying senseless on the ground, in a state of shock.

The knight raised head and arm, but his armour was so heavy he could not get up. He strained and strained, but continually fell back to the ground.

"Come to my aid!" Sir Eustace Useless cried.

But the boys were laughing so much that their imaginations failed. Knight, horse and ponies disappeared, and the boys tumbled to the earth.

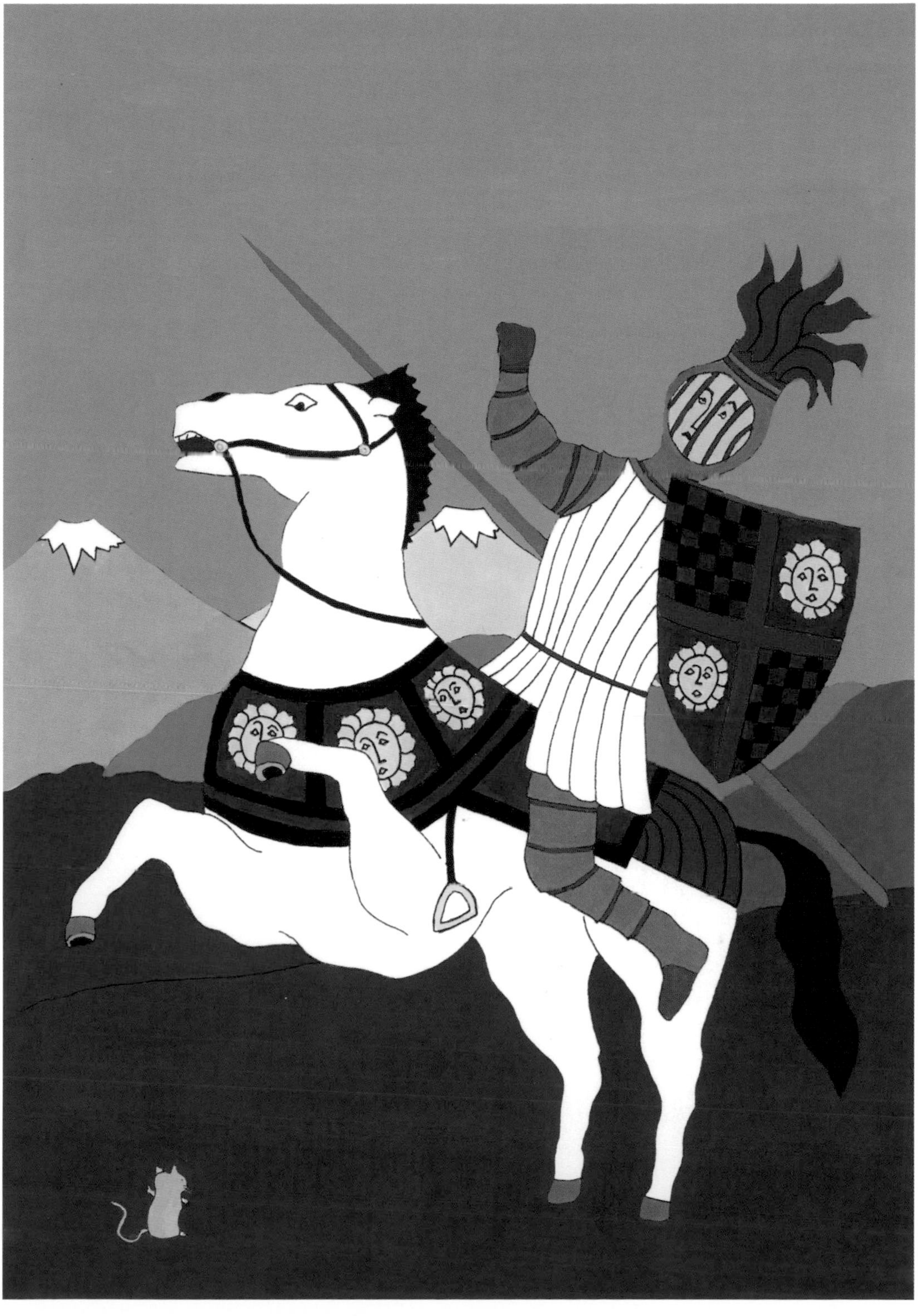

The boys began to walk. They were tired and hungry and the hills seemed to go on for ever. As they walked, Julius was deep in thought.

"If that knight came from our minds," he said at last, "perhaps if we wish hard for food and drink, food and drink will appear."

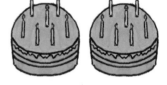

"Birthday cake," thought Alexander, wishing very hard. A birthday cake appeared at their feet.

"Birthday cakes," corrected Julius. Two more appeared.

Alexander shouted with excitement: "Biscuits! Biscuits!"

"Chocolate biscuits," corrected Julius, not satisfied with the plain assortment.

"Gallons and gallons of lemonade. To wash it down!" shouted Alexander.

A torrent of yellow liquid gushed out from between the rocks, and washed all the food down the hillside.

"You idiot! You idiot!"

"It's not my fault."

"Yes it is."

"All right. Let's wish for more food and drink."

They wished for more food and drink, but none appeared.

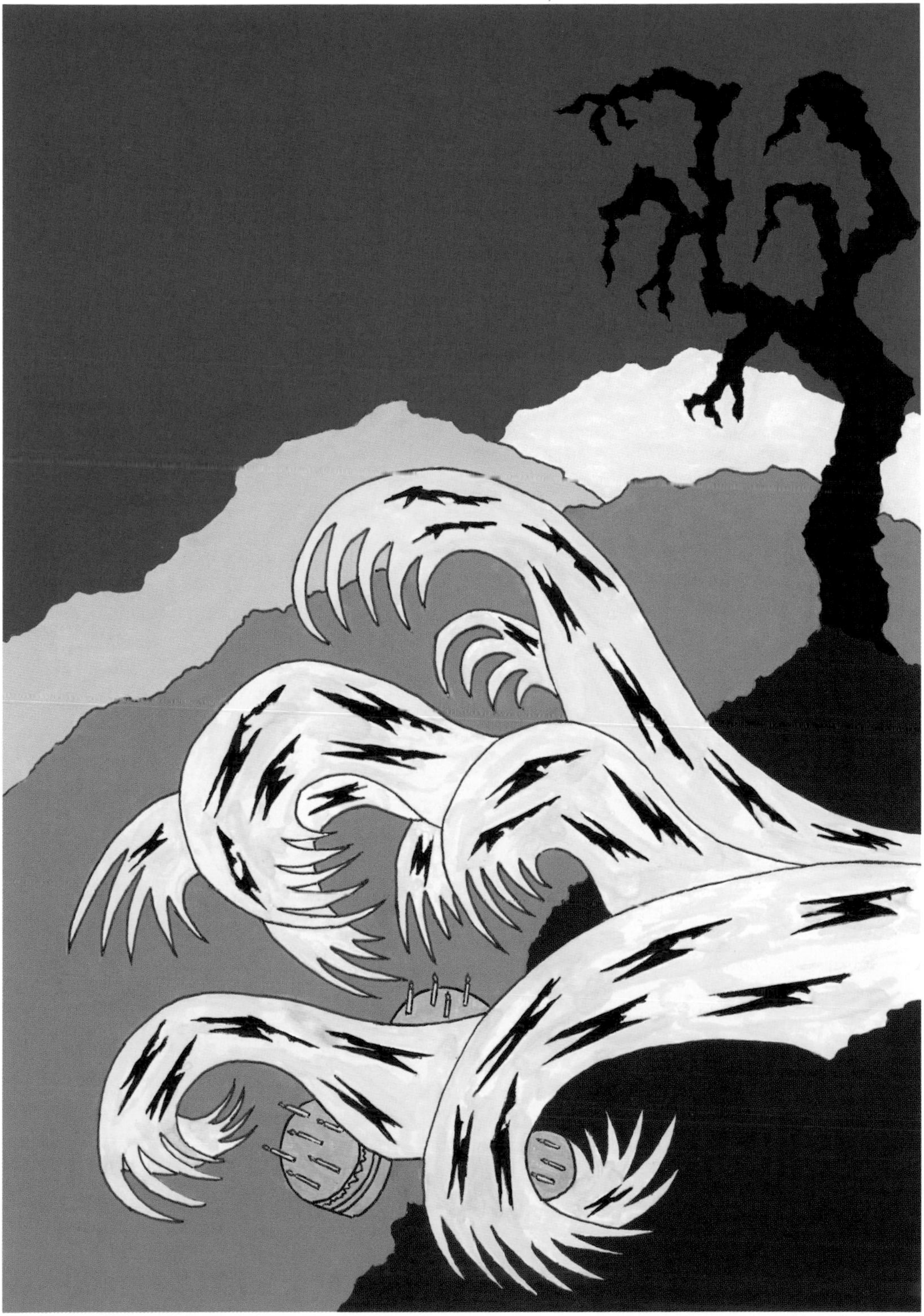

"This way!" said Julius.

"No that way!" retorted Alexander. The weather began to get colder.

"We'll never get home. We'll never find Snuggle and Benjamin." It began to rain.

"We'll starve to death. Or freeze." The wind began to howl.

"Stop it! Stop it! Stop it at once!" cried a little man in uniform, running towards them, shivering with cold.

The boys looked up, and sighed gloomily: "We're not doing anything."

"You've done it again," panted the little man.

"We haven't done a thing."

"No! No! No! One more gloomy thought and there will be snow. Told you so."

"We do not understand."

"In these hills it is the mind which controls. It even controls the weather. If you think gloomy thoughts, there is snow, or hurricane, or drought, depending on the time of year."

"That's odd."

"Very odd indeed."

"I have come to take you to the Gardener.

Quick! Follow me."

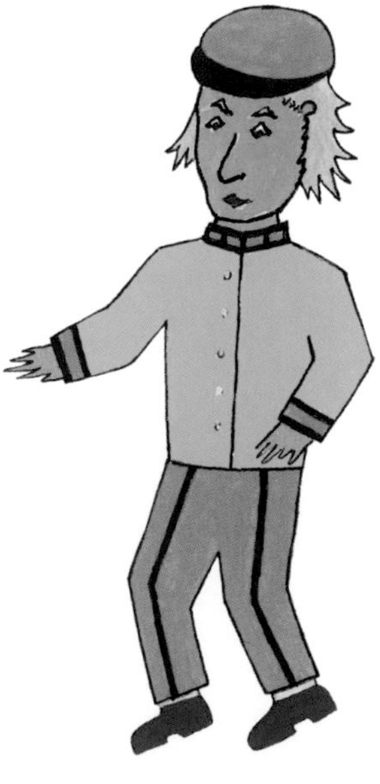

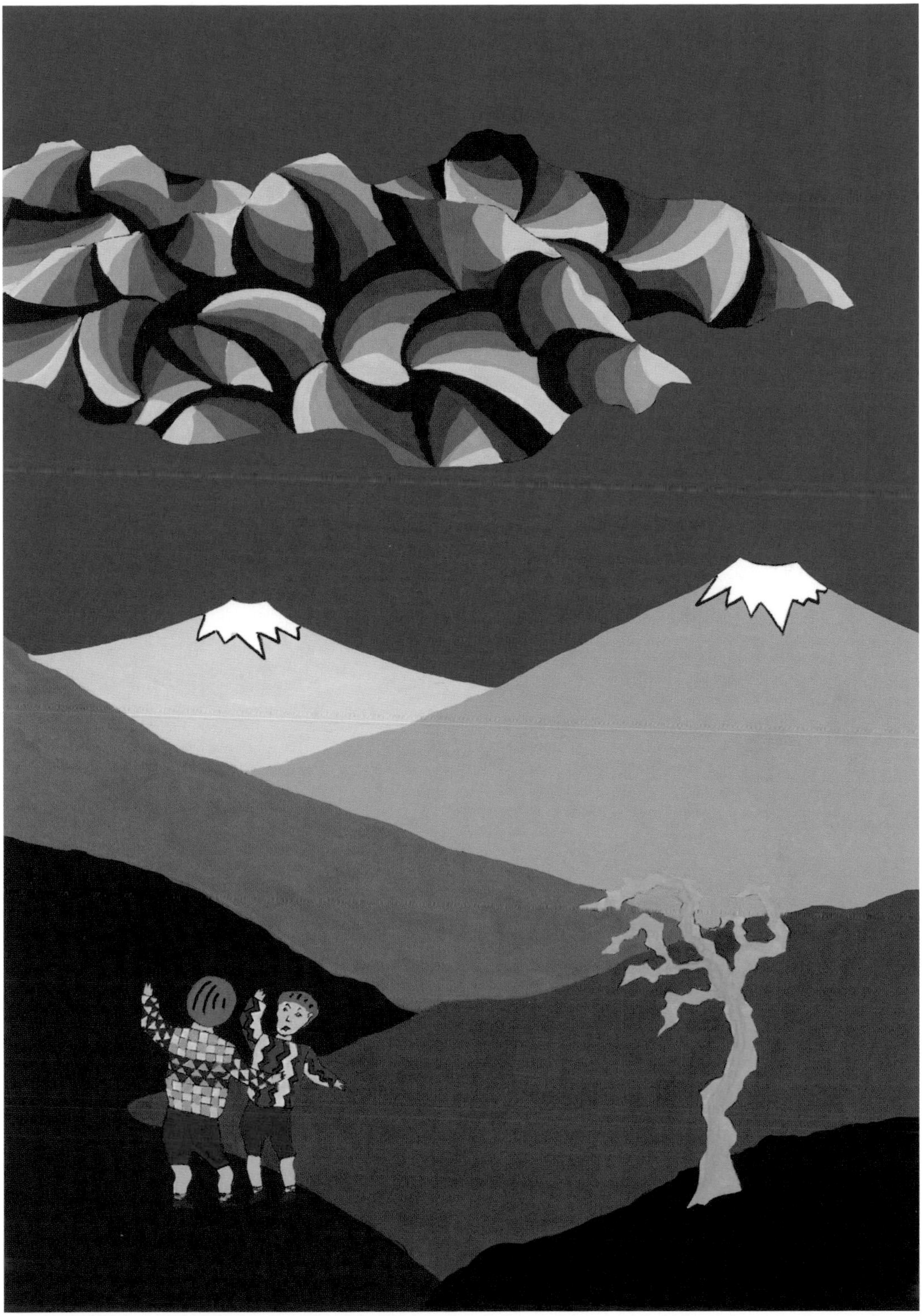

CHAPTER FIVE

Julius and Alexander followed the Guide down a gully to a valley, where he opened a door in a high brick wall. The boys went into the Garden. "The Garden is dying!" they cried in horror.

The grass was yellow, the blossom black: plants, shrubs and trees, all were dying. They hurried to the summer house in the centre of the Garden around which plants, grass and trees were still alive. They found the Gardener lying on a couch, Benjamin standing beside him.

The Gardener opened his eyes, and looked kindly at the boys. But in his eyes there was great pain.

"Listen carefully. Upon what I have to say depends the life of my kingdom.

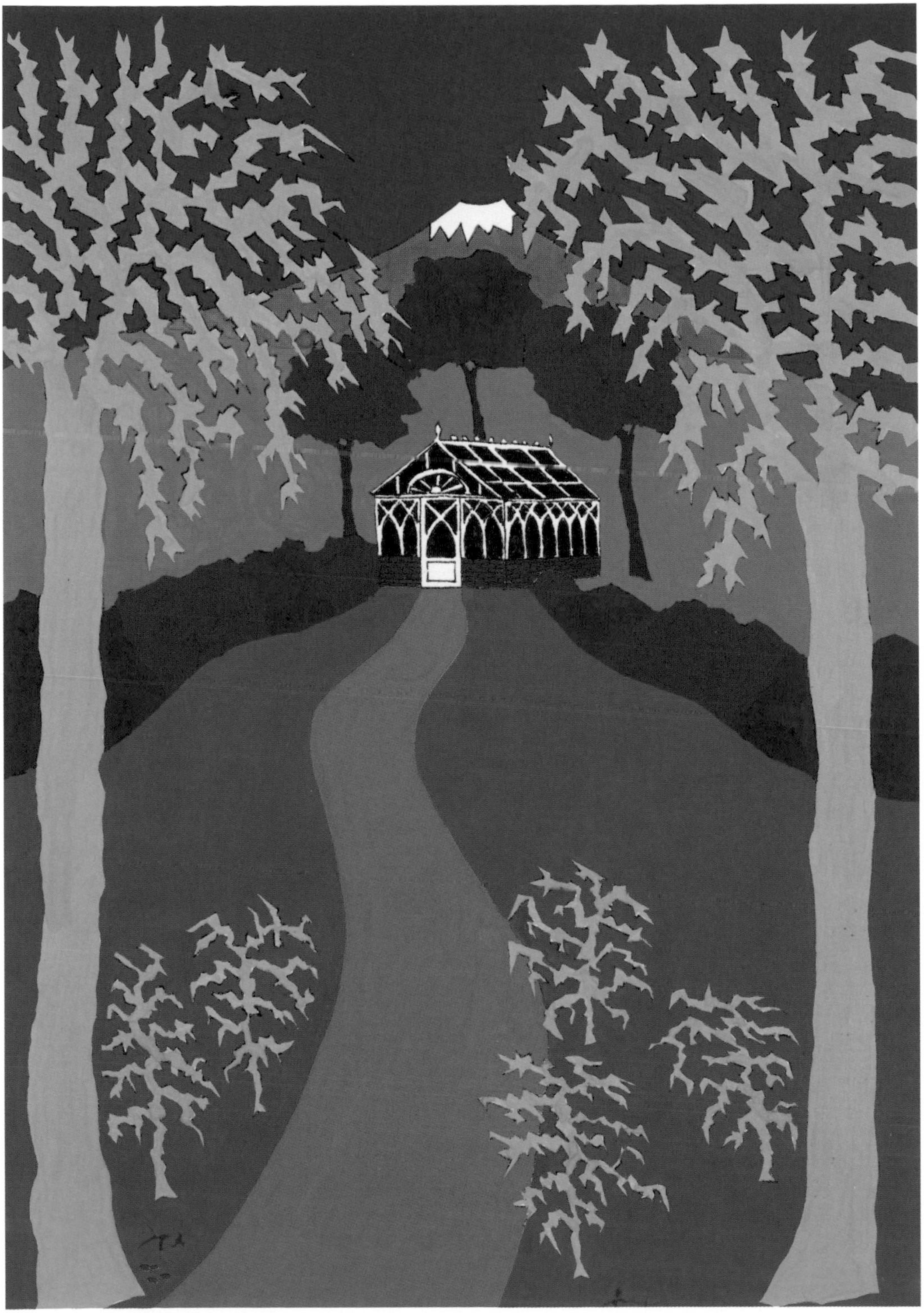

"When the witch Griselda and Snuggle fell from your world to the Land of Ramion, they were drawn by an evil power to a circle of witches. Snuggle tried to flee, but the circle bound him. In a blinding flash Griselda imprisoned Snuggle in a block of crystal. Neither dead nor alive, he suffers constant pain."

"Poor Snuggle!" cried the boys, who loved their cat.

"Griselda has placed the block of crystal in the hills above the Garden. In those hills the mind controls. I feel Snuggle's pain deep inside me. I am old, and cannot long endure, and so must die, and with me will die my garden, and with the Garden will die the Land of Ramion. I die unless Snuggle is set free."

"But how?" asked the boys.

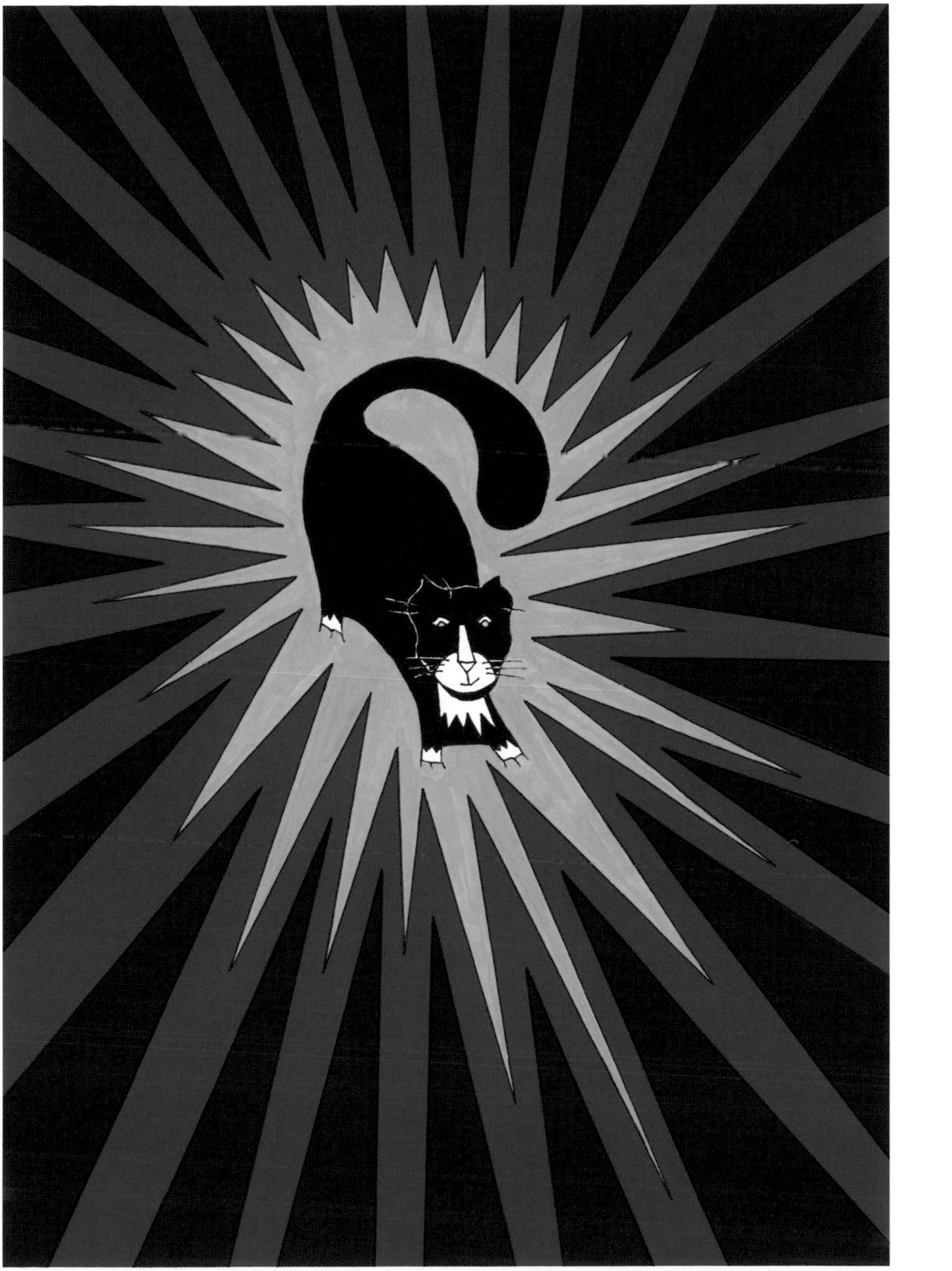

The Gardener paused and sought for strength.

"In the Crystal Kingdom far away there is a crystal key, which will unlock the block, and set Snuggle free. It is a difficult journey. You must pass through the Land of Nothingness. In that land you must not wish a single wish."

"What happens if we do?"

"You will fall into the Land of Desire."

"Is that dangerous?"

"It depends upon what you wished. Are you prepared to go?"

"We would do anything to save Snuggle," replied the boys. "And you of course," they added.

With those words the boys disappeared, fell and fell through the void, and landed in a muddled heap, limbs all tangled up in nothingness. In that land nothing had substance, all was mist in different shades of swirling grey.

As Julius stepped forward to help Benjamin up, he fell through both Benjamin and Alexander, and coming out the other side, cried in surprise: "Our bodies have turned to nothingness."

They floated, hardly able to distinguish between different shades of grey, where a foot or arm ended, and the ground or sky began. If by mistake they met a tree or rock of solid mist, their bodies swirled around it.

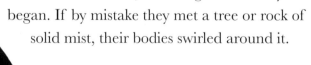

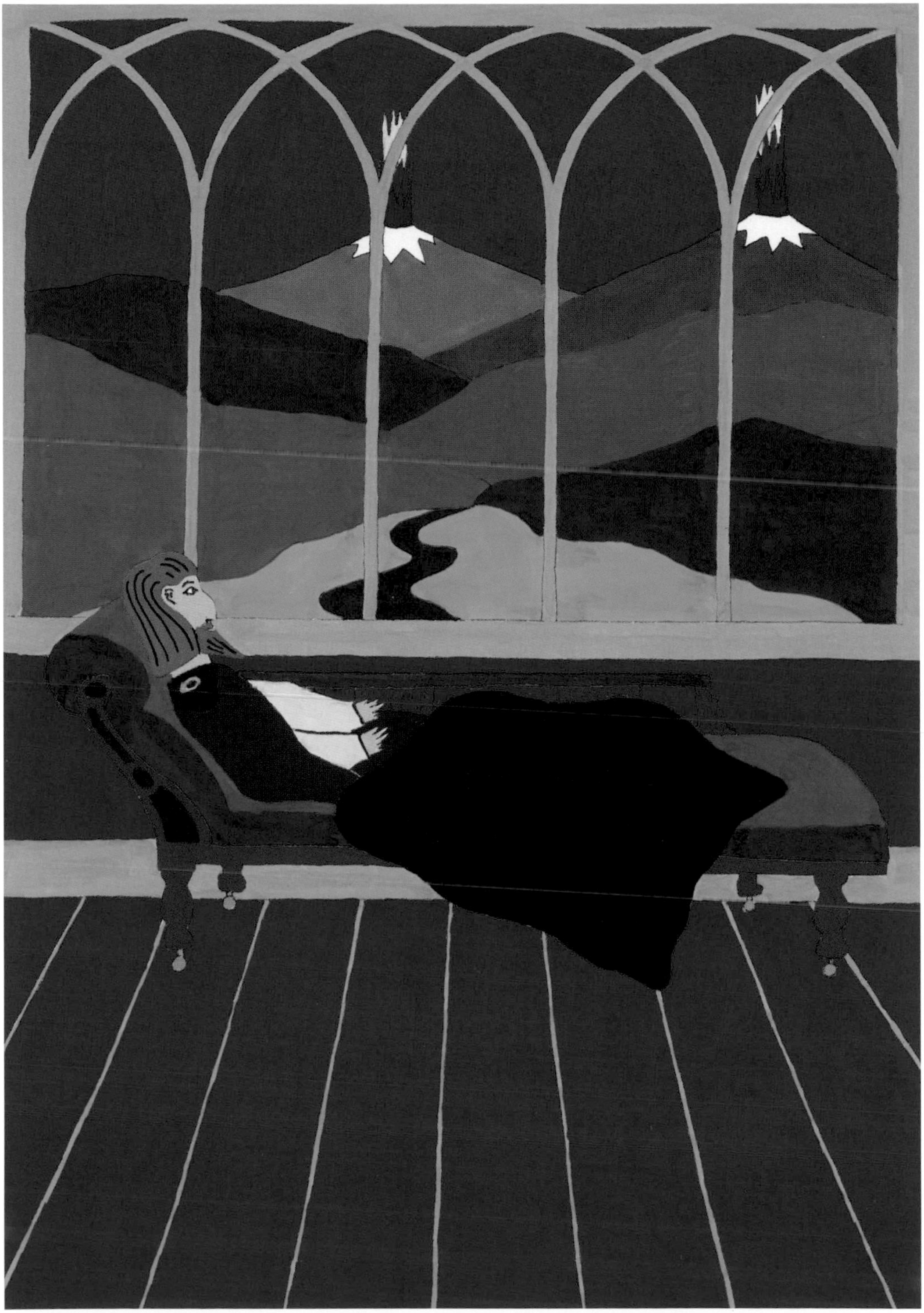

"Remember," said Julius. "Do not wish for anything."

The boys had not travelled far, when out of the mist there rode a princess of swirling shades of black and grey, upon a horse of nothingness. Behind her ran two yapping dogs of swirling mist.

"Young sirs! Welcome to my kingdom! Julius! Benjamin! Run behind with the dogs. Master Alexander! You can ride with me."

Julius and Benjamin went behind, grumbling softly, as the two dogs swirled and yelped around their feet. Alexander got up on the horse behind the Princess.

"Master Alexander, you are a boy of beauty. You are fit to grace a royal palace. In my palace you will sit beside me. Servants will bring you food and drink." Then she added with great cunning: "What would you like to eat?"

Before Alexander could stop himself, he wished a wish. The Princess of the Night gave a horrid laugh as the boys disappeared.

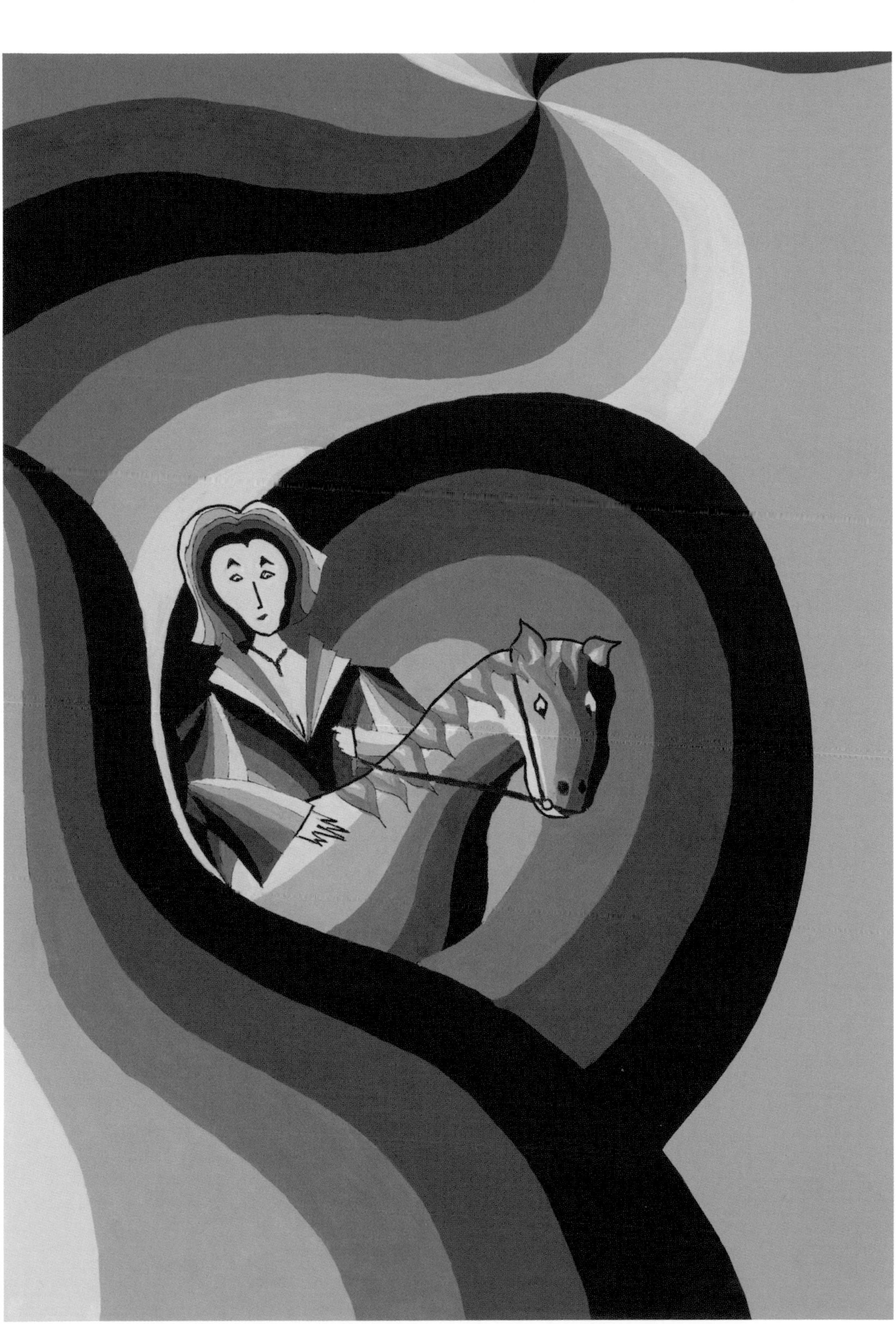

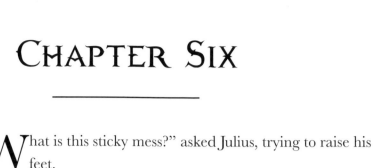

CHAPTER SIX

"What is this sticky mess?" asked Julius, trying to raise his feet.

Benjamin bent down, stuck a finger in the ground, put it to his lips, and exclaimed in surprise, "It's icing!"

Slowly the boys trudged through the icing, oozing sticky up to their knees. In the distance they could see a tall, lilac pillar. On the pillar was a bright flame.

"I can see another," said Julius.

"And another and another and another," added Benjamin.

Alexander did not say a thing. They reached a dark ridge of icing. "It's an A," said Julius. Turning, he shouted, "Alexander! Did you wish a wish?" Alexander mumbled. He looked down at the ground. "It's your birthday cake." Reluctantly, Alexander agreed.

At that moment Scrooey-Looey walked towards them. "What are you doing here?" asked Benjamin in surprise (for back at The Old Vicarage Scrooey-Looey was a glove puppet who lived on the top shelf in the nursery).

"I was eating a huge lettuce when suddenly this cake appeared. What idiot wished a wish?" asked the rabbit. Julius and Benjamin pointed at Alexander, who made a wish to disappear, but nothing happened. "You idiot! You lunatic! You cretinous lump of lard!"

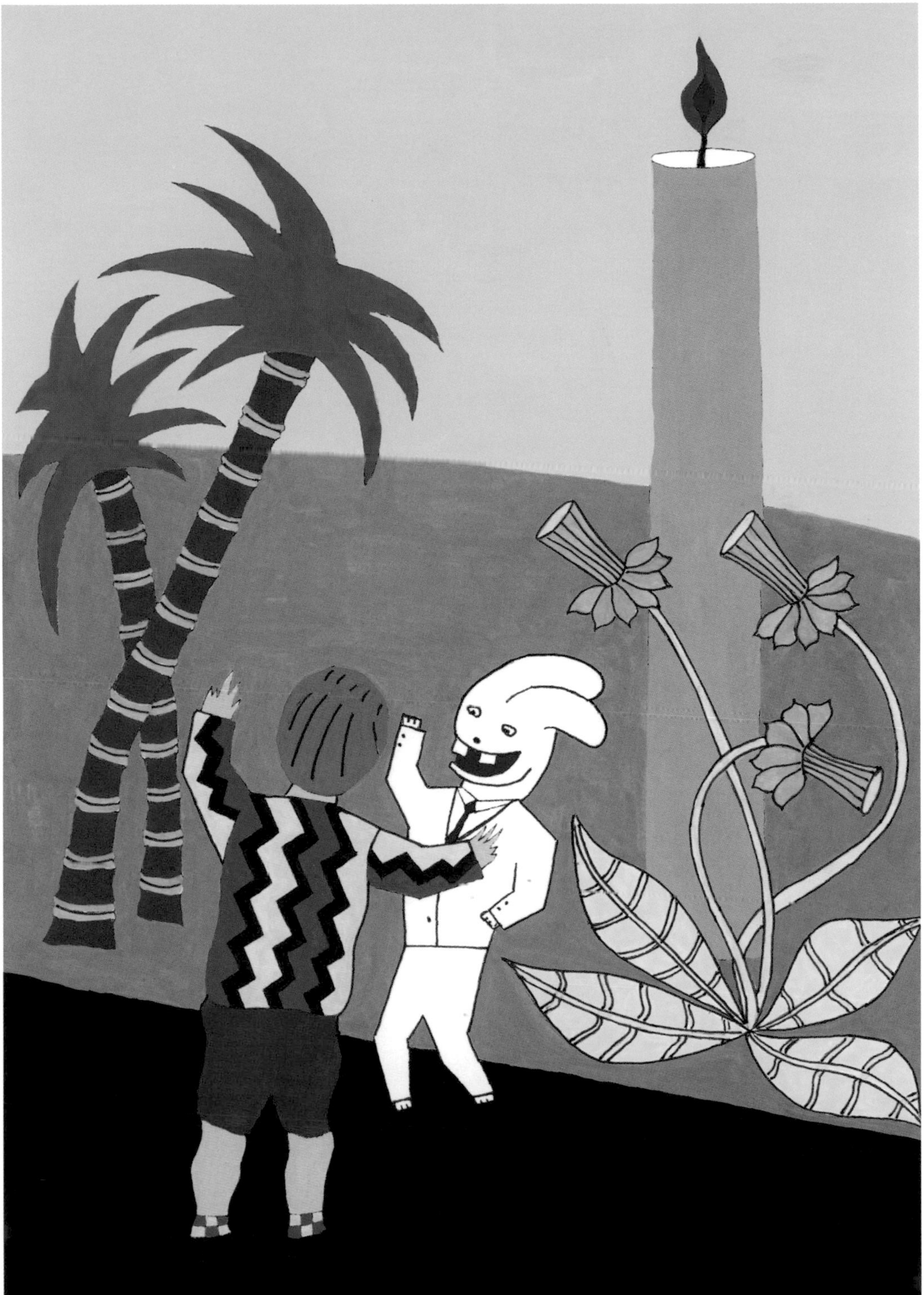

Just then a giraffe ran past. Julius and Benjamin looked up in surprise. Then there was a fearsome roar. Scrooey-Looey began to tremble, and hid behind the nearest candle.

"Alexander! What sort of birthday cake did you wish for?" asked Julius.

"A jungle cake."

"What sort of animals?" "The normal sort."

"What sort?" "Monkeys and giraffes."

"Any others?" "Lions and tigers."

"Lions and tigers!" shrieked Scrooey-Looey, coming out from behind the candle, and jumping up into Benjamin's arms. But Benje was too small, and they fell backwards in the icing. There was another fearsome roar.

"Help! Help!" cried Benjamin. "I'm stuck. Get off me, Scrooey-Looey!"

His brothers pulled them out of the icing. There was another fearsome roar, and all ran (which was not easy through icing oozing sticky up to their knees) until they reached the edge of the cake.

"It's a high cliff!"

"We'll never get down there!"

"We're trapped!"

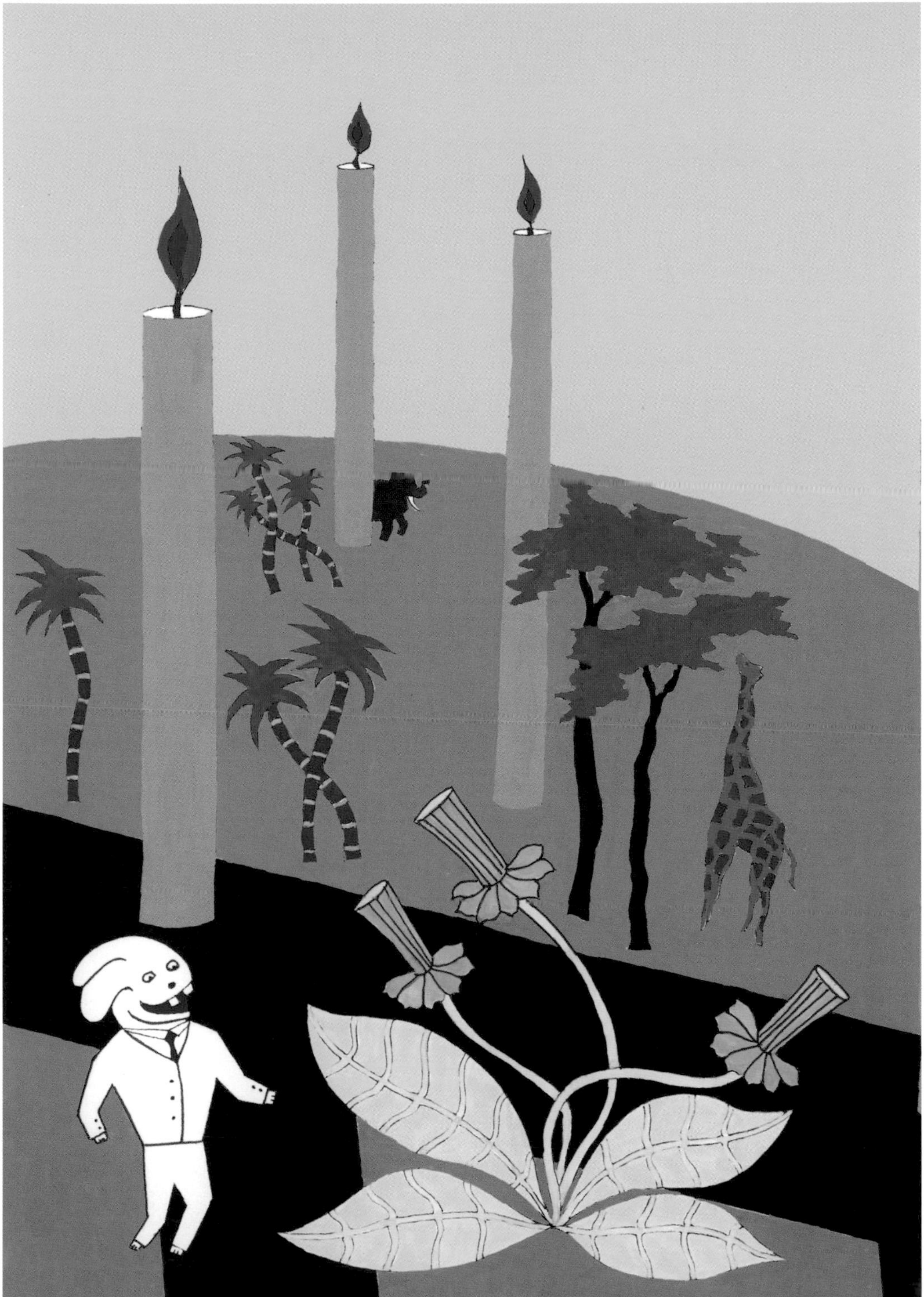

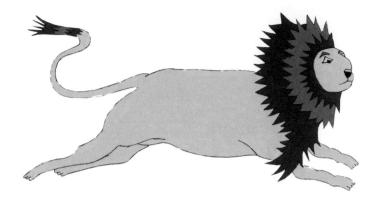

Scrooey-Looey screamed: "Look! There's the lion." The lion was creeping through the icing.

"Quick, quick," said Julius, "push the candle over." They pushed the candle over. It fell propped up against the side of the cake, and the flame went out. There was another fearsome roar.

"I'll go first," said Julius sitting astride the candle, and sliding off the cake to the ground below.

"Weee!" shouted Alexander, following close behind.

"Oh help!" cried Scrooey-Looey. "I'm scared of heights." There was another fearsome roar.

"Come on Scrooey-Looey. I'll hold you tight," said Benjamin. Scrooey-Looey sat astride the candle with Benjamin behind him holding him tight. There was another fearsome roar, as the lion came bounding towards them.

"Go! Go! Go!" shouted Julius and Alexander from far below.

Benje gave Scrooey-Looey a gentle push, and the two slid down the candle.

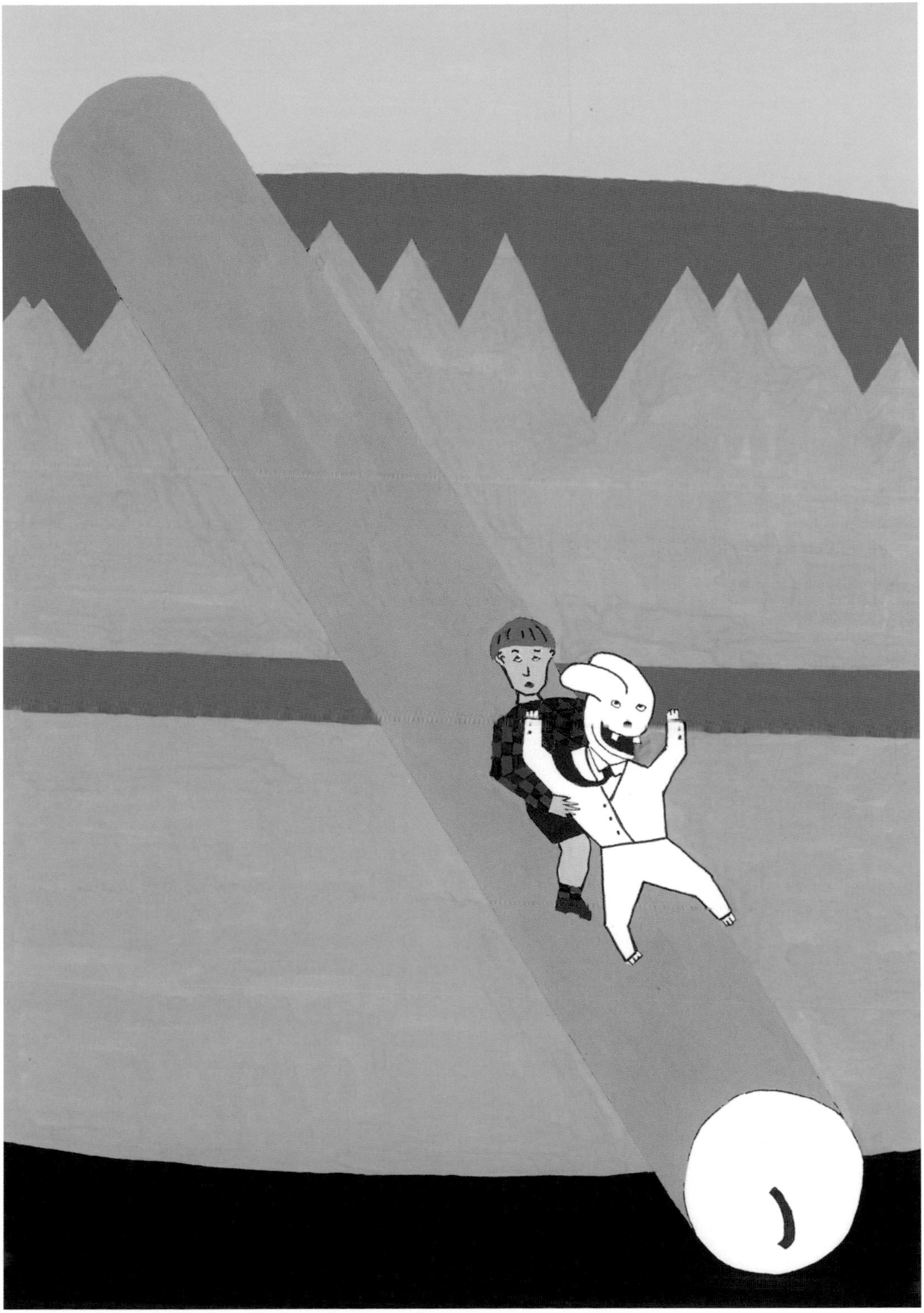

As Scrooey-Looey looked about him he gave a squeal of delight: they had landed in a forest of lettuces and carrots fifty foot high. "Great! Great! Great! More! More! More!" he shouted, as he began to eat.

The rabbit did not see the hairy caterpillar, twenty foot long, two foot wide and high, until its jaws began to close around his head.

"Look out! Scrooey-Looey!" shouted Benjamin, pushing the rabbit out of the way, just as the jaws snapped shut.

The four ran and ran. The caterpillar was only just behind them, with jaws open wide, when a lion leapt out in front of them.

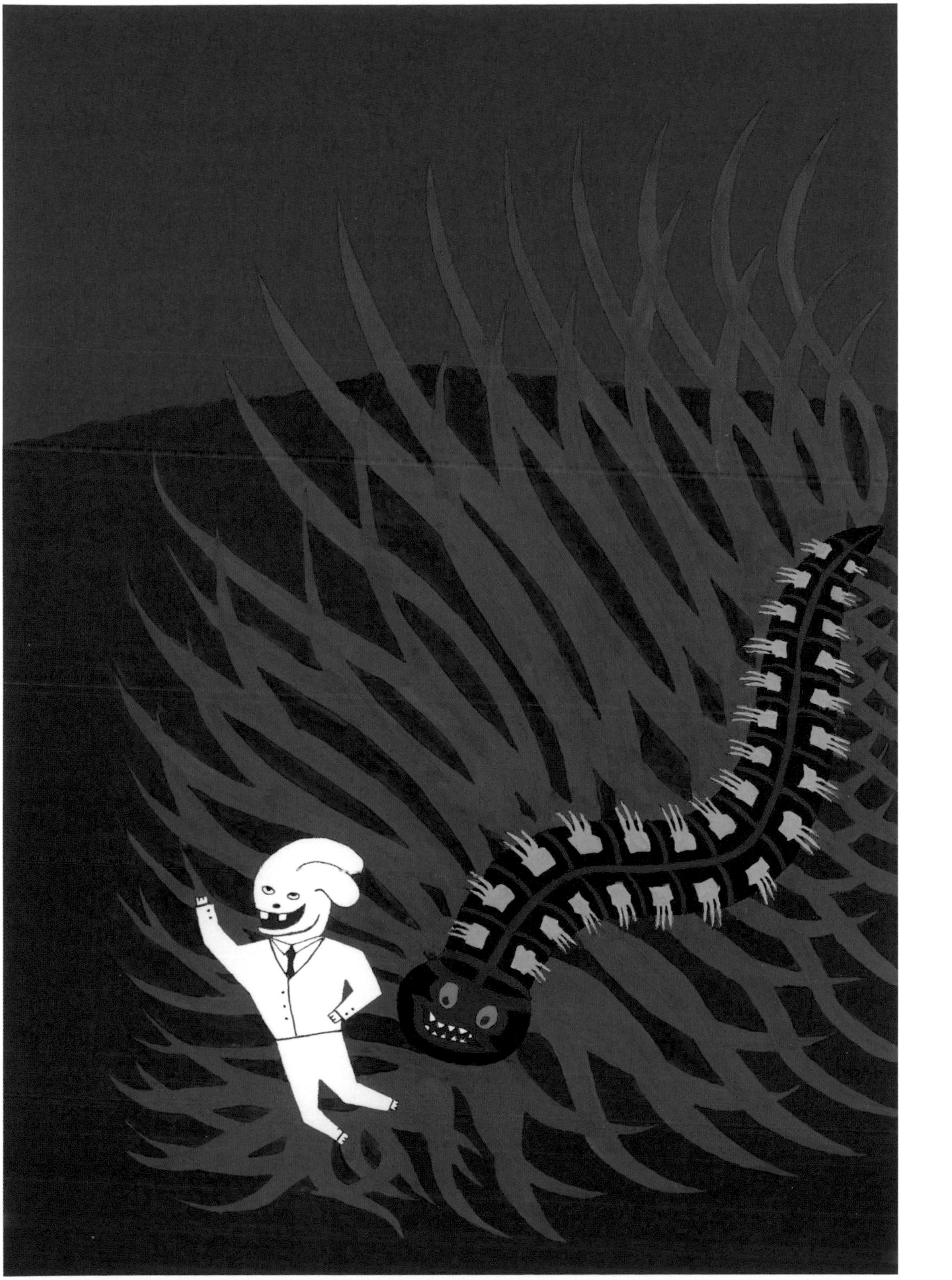

"Help! It's going to eat us!" screamed the boys.

"No I'm not," softly roared the Lion of Icing.

"But you chased us off the cake."

"Did you want to be stuck in icing for ever? Quick, get up on my back."

Boys and rabbit climbed on the lion's back, and giving a roar, the lion ran and ran, leaving the caterpillar far behind. Then it began to rain. The rain soaked into the body of the Lion of Icing, and he began to melt away.

"I can carry you no further," softly roared the Lion of Icing, as the boys and rabbit slipped to the ground. The lion disappeared, and the rain washed the icing into the earth.

Then Julius spied a cavern. "Quick! Let's hide." They hurried in out of the rain. In one wall there was a vein of crystal.

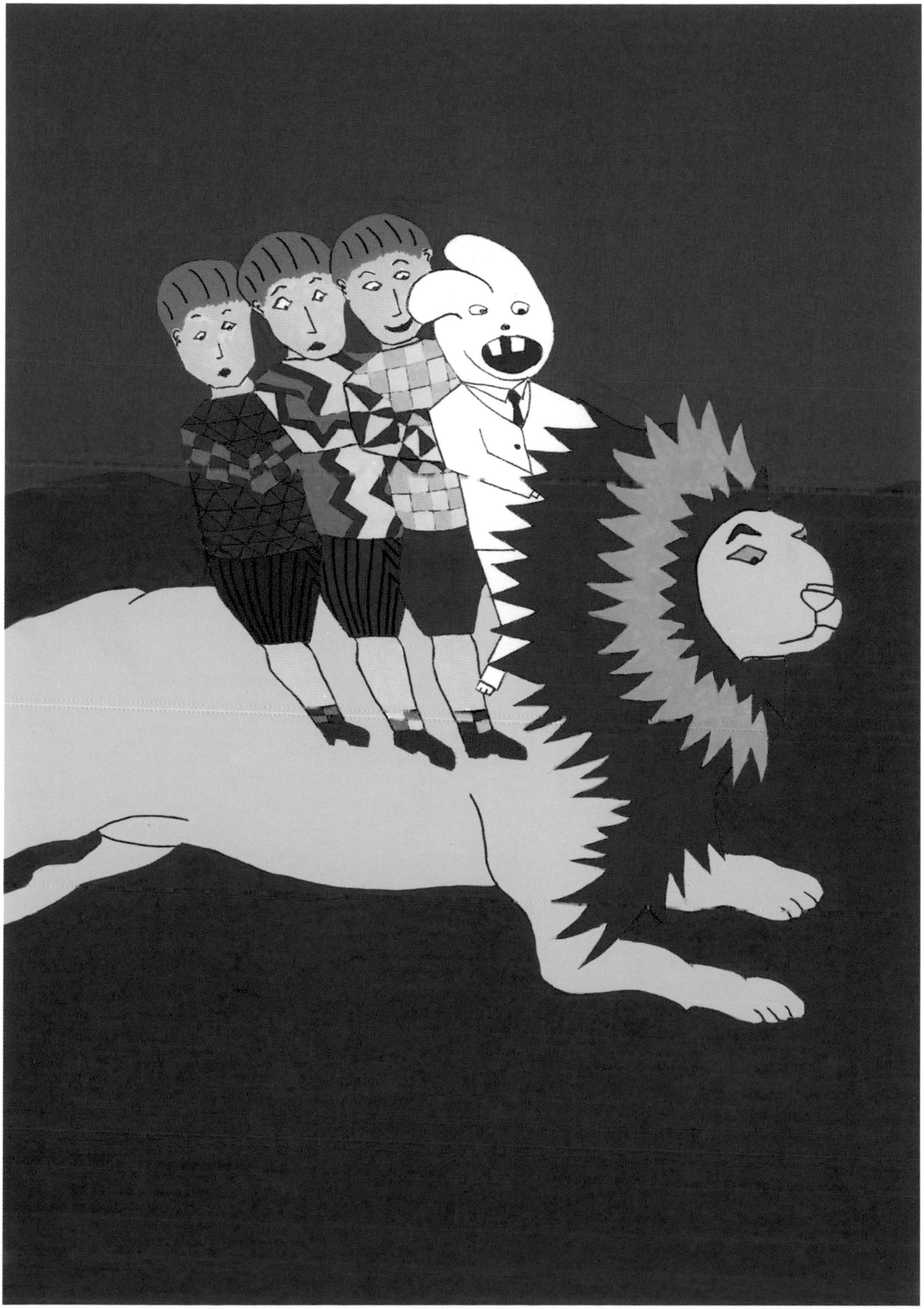

CHAPTER SEVEN

The boys and rabbit wandered through the cavern until they met a huge slug reading in his library. "You can go no further unless you tell me a story," said the slug. He turned to Benjamin. "What story can you tell?"

"Once upon a time…" But then he stopped for Benjamin was little, and not very good at telling stories.

The slug turned to Scrooey-Looey. "Er. Once upon a time there was some lettuce…"

"Stop!" cried the slug. "I'm tired of lettuce. You four will go no further. You have no imagination."

"I can tell a story," replied Julius.

"You can. Well begin."

"Once upon a time …"

"We've had that bit. Get on with the story."

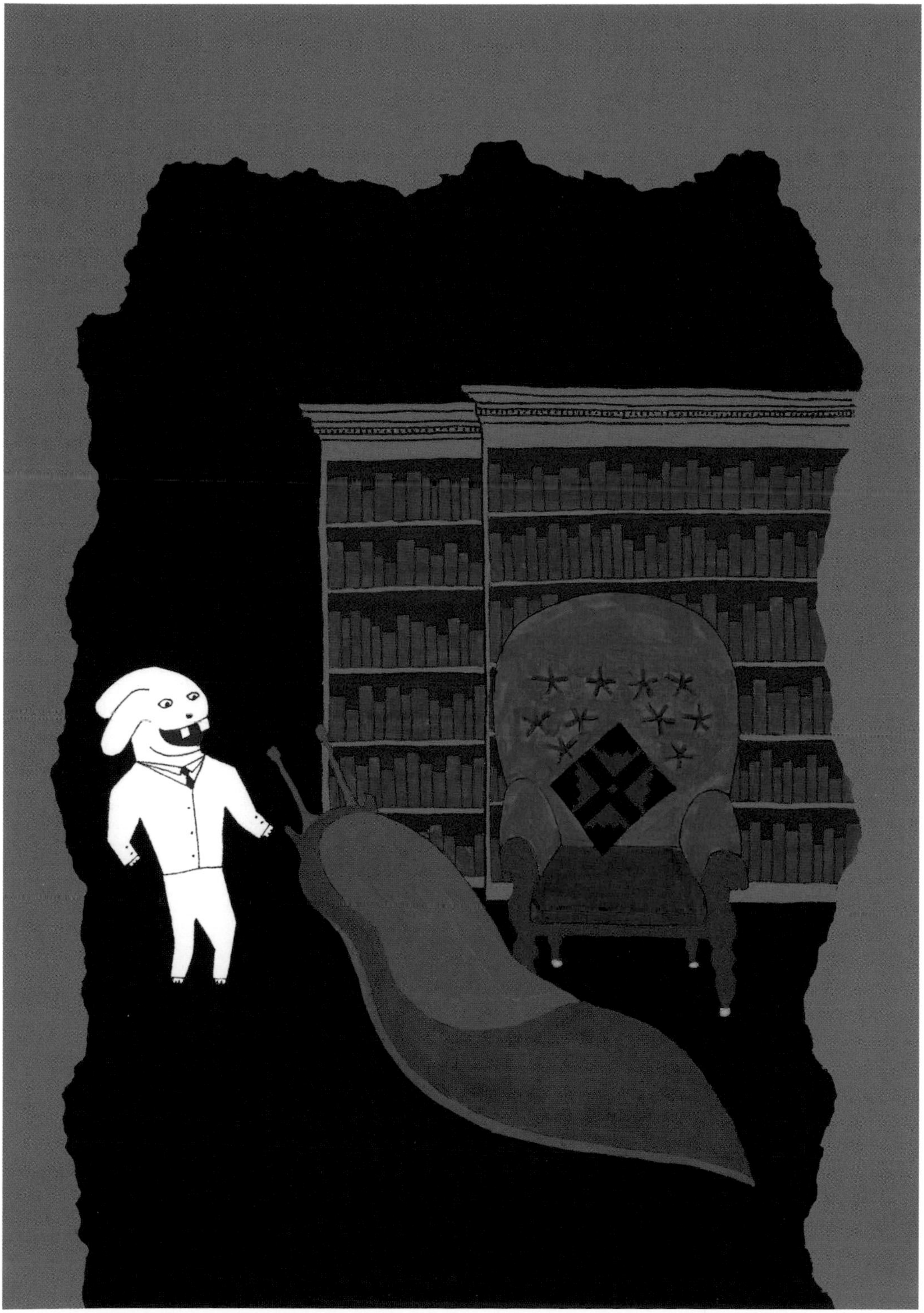

"In the far reaches of the Land of Ramion there lived a great green scaly monster called Ravenous. He was a very fussy eater. He only ate little boys called Benjamin."

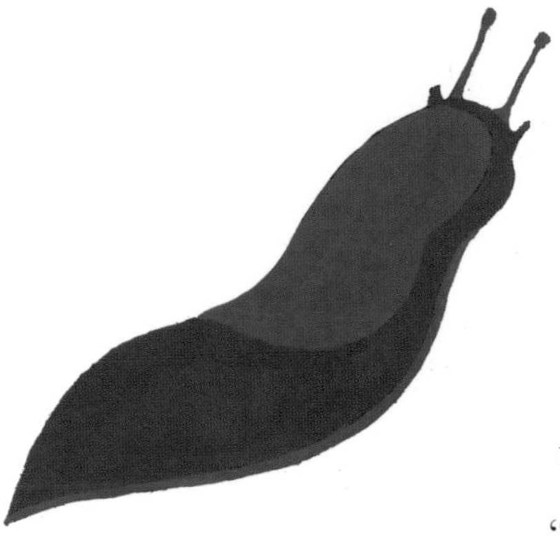

"Why Benjamin?" protested Benjamin. "Why not little boys called Julius?"

"There weren't enough of them."

"That's not fair. Why not little boys called Alexander?"

"Silence!" boomed the slug. "I want to hear the story. Continue boy."

"Well," said Julius, "whenever Ravenous met a little boy, he cocked his head to one side, and tried to smile politely (which is difficult if you are great green and scaly).

"What is your name little boy?" asked Ravenous.

"Peter sir."

"Are you sure?" sighed Ravenous unhappily, his stomach rumbling.

"Yes sir."

"You're sure you're not a Benjamin."

"Oh no sir."

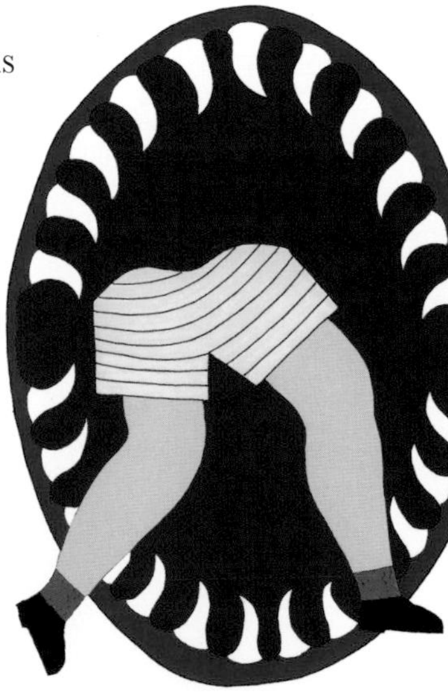

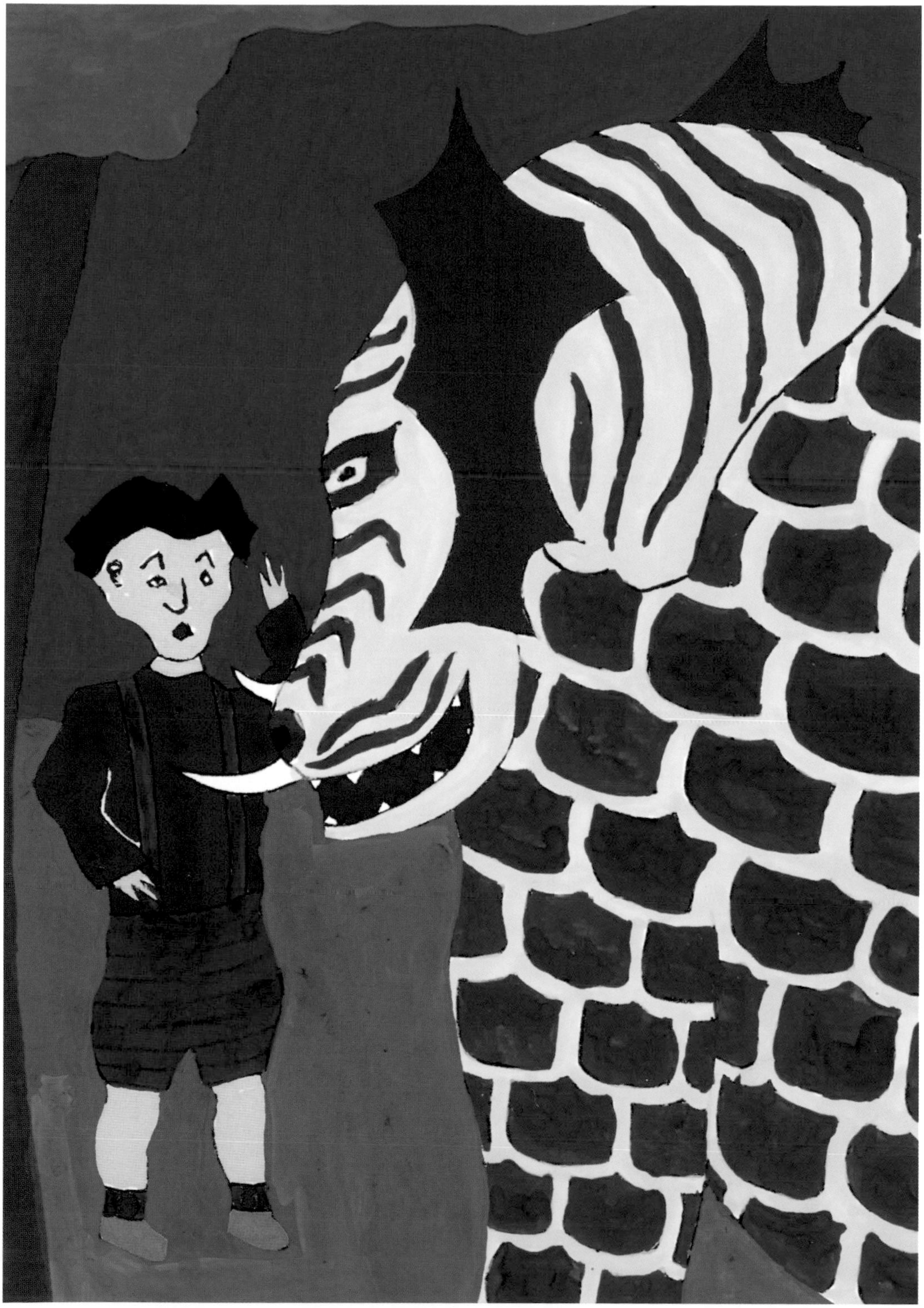

"Ravenous sighed and went on his way. But when Ravenous met a little boy called Benjamin, he sucked his blood, chomped his flesh and spat out the bones."

"I hate this story!" shouted Benjamin. "It's not fair. Why am I always eaten?"

"Silence! Continue boy."

"Ravenous did not lead a happy life. Other monsters were fat and jolly. Ravenous was thin and hungry. His friends told him not to be so silly.

"Little boys called Rupert and Mark taste just as good."

"Why not eat little girls called Benjamina?"

"No! No!" snorted Ravenous, stamping his foot. "I will not eat anything but little boys called Benjamin."

"Until there came the dreadful day, when in the whole Land of Ramion there was not a single boy left called Benjamin. Word had got around that if mothers and fathers called their children Benjamin, the monster Ravenous would come along, suck their blood, chomp their flesh and spit out the bones.

"I'm not having that!" cried the mothers. "We'll call the baby Albert instead."

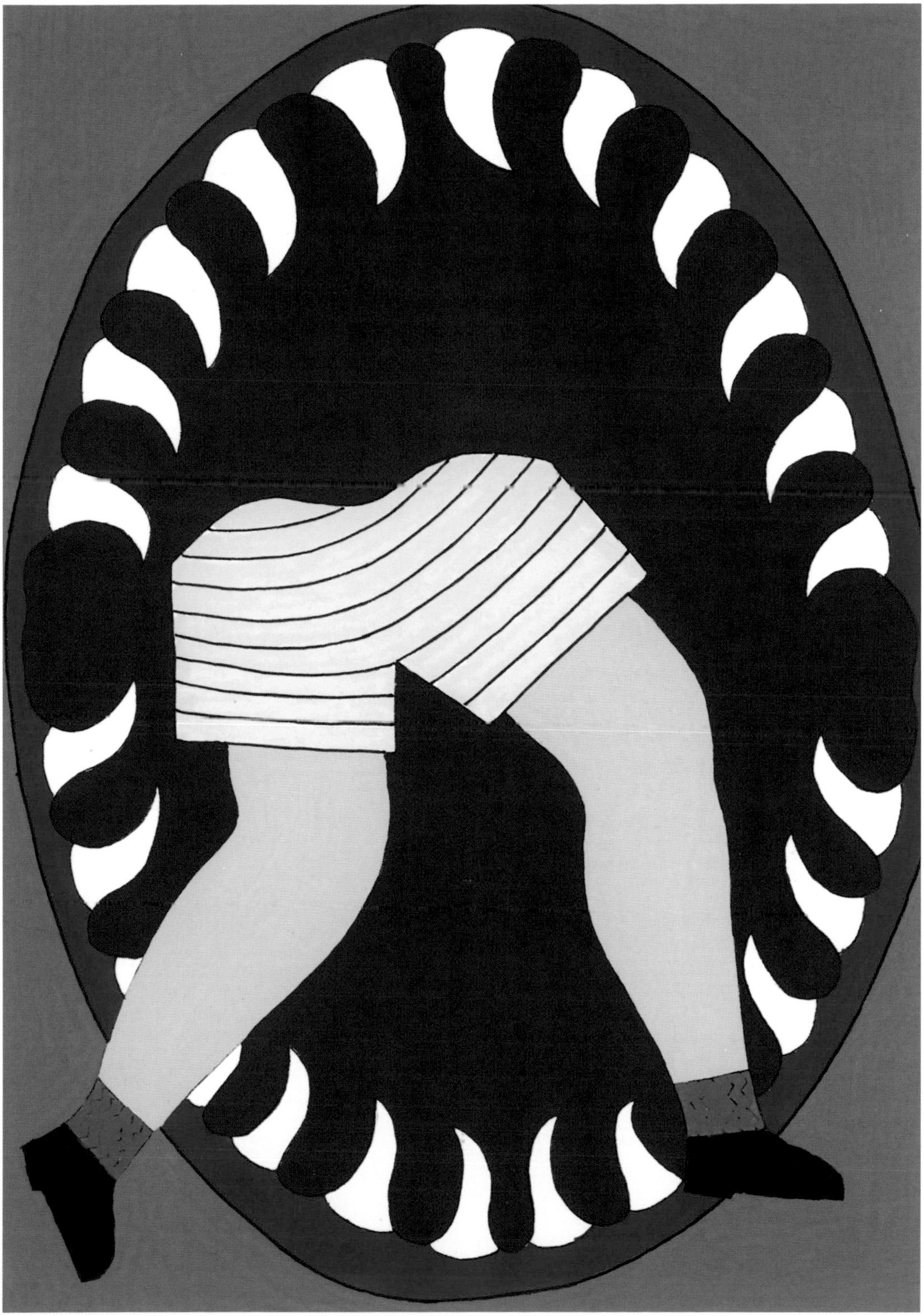

"Ravenous got thinner and thinner. He got more and more miserable.

"What's your name little boy?" asked Ravenous.

"Albert sir," came the reply.

"Ravenous turned and stomped away. But one day Ravenous was talking to an old woman, and she told him that three boys had come to the Land of Ramion, called Julius, Alexander and Benjamin. Hungrily Ravenous tried to find the boys. He was shocked when he learnt that the boys had returned home to Shoreham. Ravenous went to see the local magician.

"Tell me Max," said Ravenous to the magician. "How do I get to earth? To the village of Shoreham."

"It will cost you a lot of money."

"How much?"

"Ten rhyalls."

"That was a great sum of money, more than a thousand years' pocket money. But by this time Ravenous was really really hungry. So he sold his cave to another monster, and brought the money to the magician. The magician worked his deepest magic. In a flash Ravenous travelled through the void to The Old Vicarage garden.

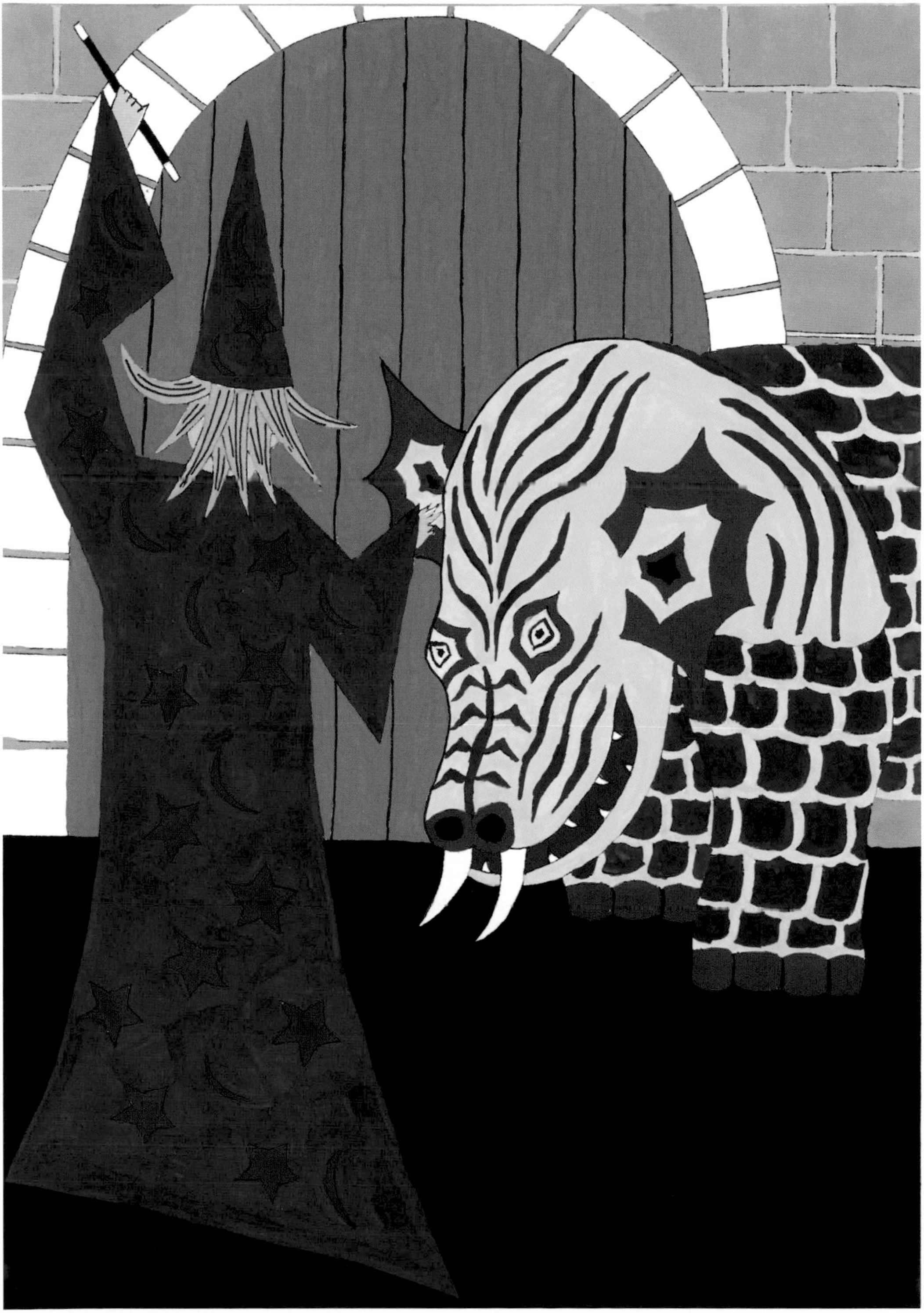

"Ravenous landed in a flower bed. Dad was very cross.

"Get off the flower bed, you great green scaly monster!" shouted Dad, shaking a hoe in rage. "You'll smash the dahlias."

"I beg your pardon," cried Ravenous politely. "I am looking for the boys."

"Dad pointed to the top of the garden, and returned to hoeing the weeds. Ravenous ambled up the garden. When he saw three boys playing in the mud, he got very excited, but remembering his manners, he cocked his head to one side, and asked the biggest boy politely, "What is your name little boy?"

"Julius."

"Ravenous was disappointed. He turned to the middle sized boy.

"What's your name little boy?"

"Alexander," came the reply.

"Ravenous was very disappointed. He turned to the littlest boy."

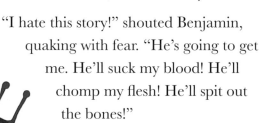

"I hate this story!" shouted Benjamin, quaking with fear. "He's going to get me. He'll suck my blood! He'll chomp my flesh! He'll spit out the bones!"

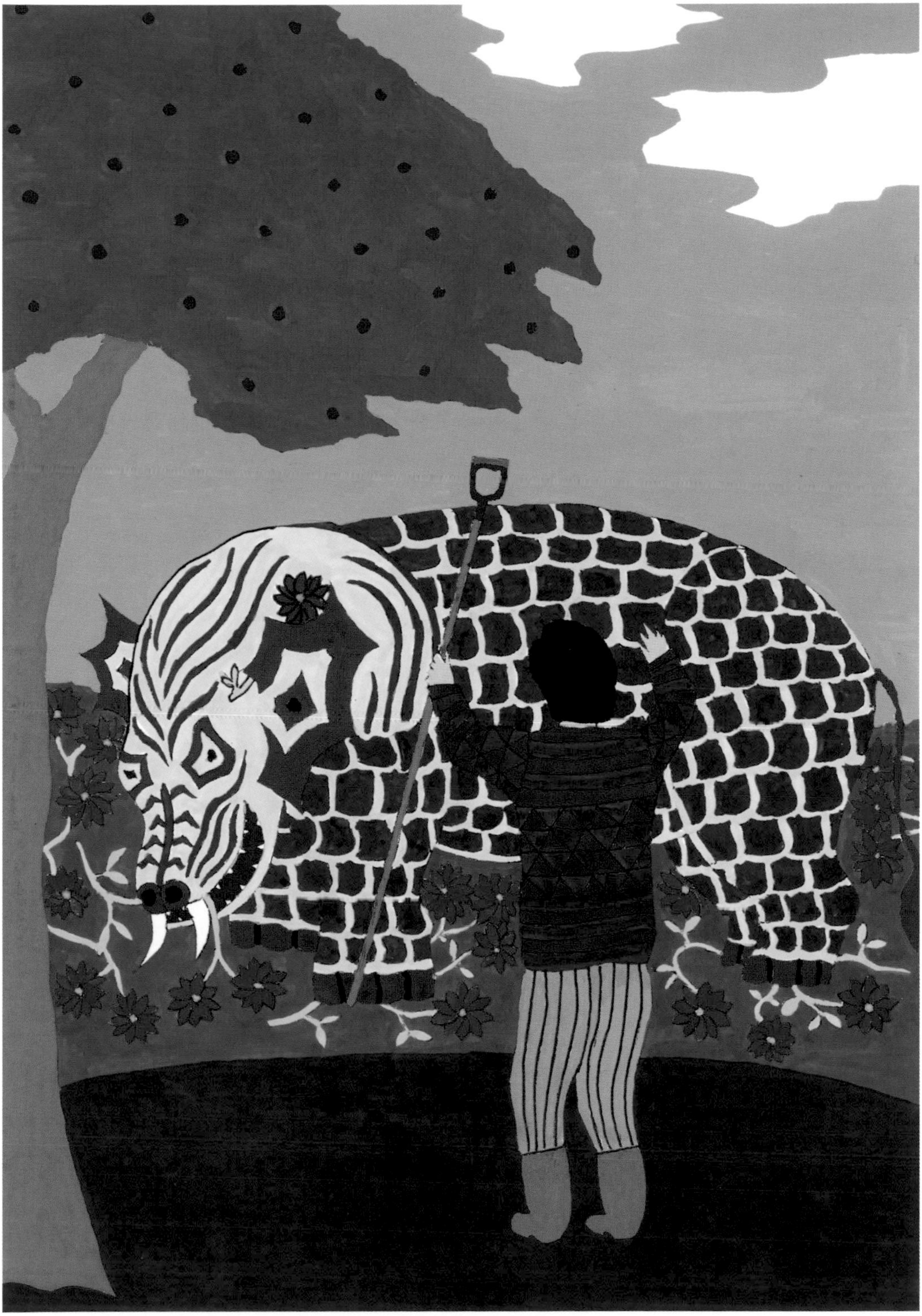

"Well," said Julius. "Ravenous turned to the littlest boy.

"What's your name little boy?" he asked.

"Now, Benjamin had heard about Ravenous. He thought hard. Swiftly he gave the monster his middle name. "Stewart," he replied.

"Are you sure?" asked Ravenous very very disappointed. "You look like a Benjamin to me. I can tell if you are lying."

"No! No!" cried Benjamin firmly. "My name is Stewart."

"Ravenous was very very very disappointed. He was also very hungry. He had not eaten for months. He thought to himself, "Perhaps I have been a little silly. Perhaps Stewarts taste as good as Benjamins. I had better find out."

"I hate this story!"

"Silence! Continue boy."

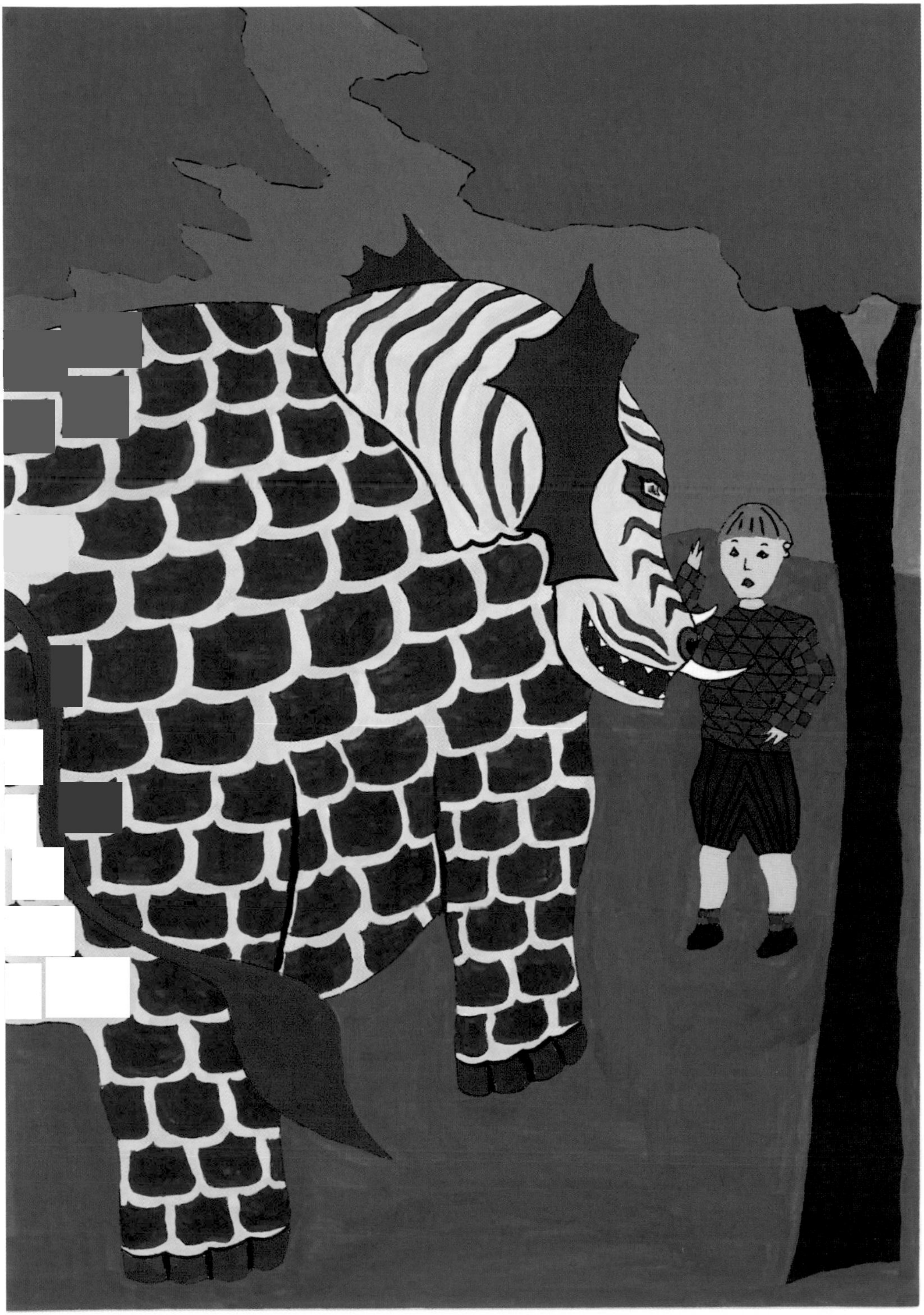

"Ravenous was about to suck the little boy's blood, chomp his flesh, spit out the bones, and find out if Stewarts tasted as good as Benjamins, when Scrooey-Looey ran up. Scrooey-Looey took one look at the great green monster, and shouted, "You scaly twit! Turnip nose!"

"Ravenous was a very serious monster. He was accustomed to being treated with respect. When Scrooey-Looey called him a scaly twit, something snapped deep inside. Ravenous exploded into a thousand bits, covering the dahlias with blood and gunge. Dad was not pleased. He waved the hoe above his head, and shouted at the boys, "Clear up that mess!"

"That's the end of the story."

"Hmmmm. The ending was a bit sudden. But the story was not bad. Not bad at all," murmured the slug. "Very well you can continue on your journey."

"That story was horrid!" grumbled Benjamin, as the boys and rabbit walked deeper into the cavern.

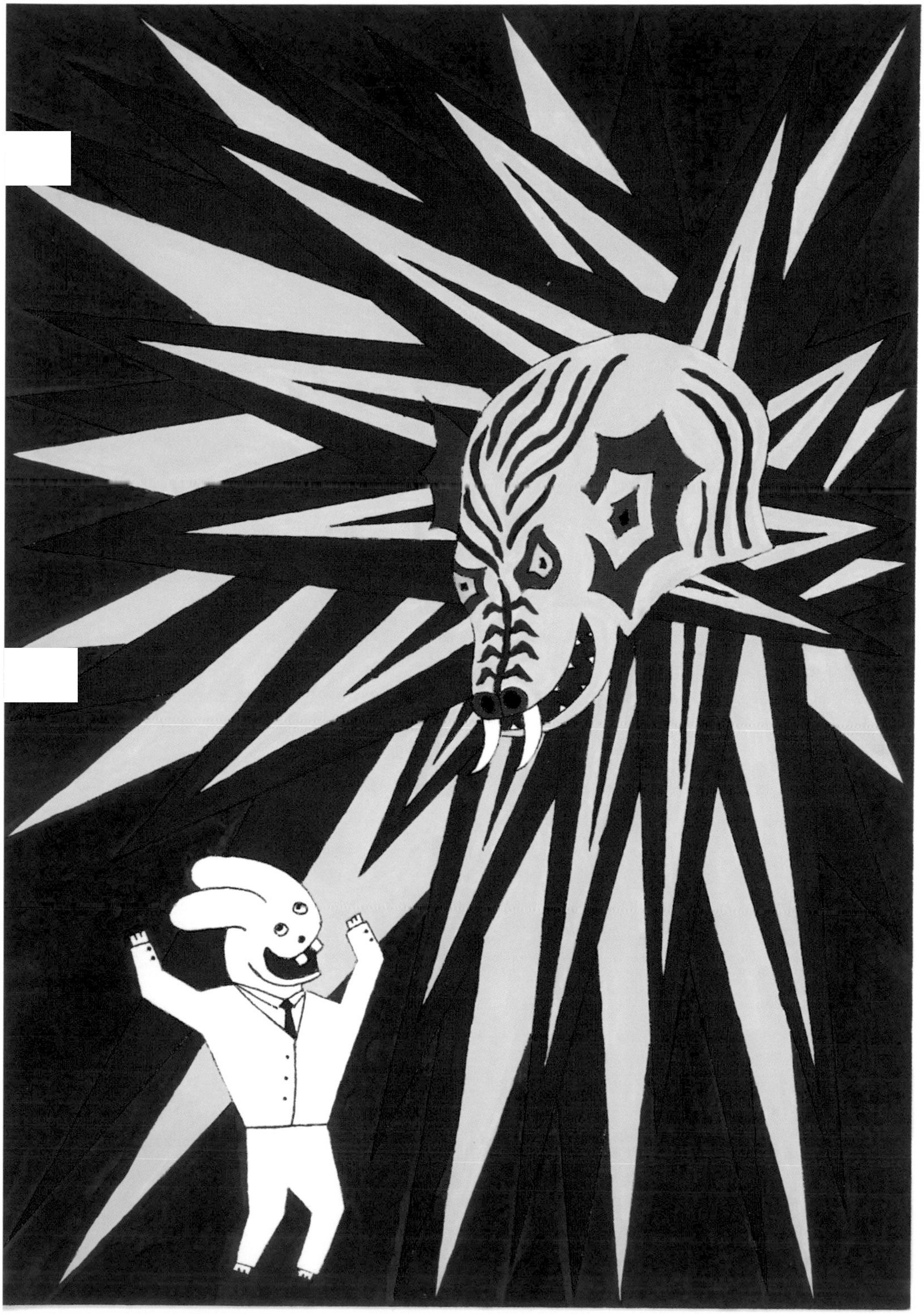

CHAPTER EIGHT

D eep within the cavern the boys and rabbit met a flamingo in pale blue cloak and wide brimmed hat holding a chisel. He stood before them wing on hip.

"My dears, you can go no further unless you give me a sculpture."

"I'll carve my initials on the wall," said Scrooey-Looey, picking up a chisel.

The flamingo gave a little scream. "Stop that rabbit!" Then he turned to the boys. "Has no one got a sculpture?" Julius and Benjamin shook their heads. "Then you cannot pass."

But Alexander looked through his pockets, and took out a special stone he had found in the garden of The Old Vicarage. "If you look at this stone from one side, it is a lion's claw, from another the tooth of a dinosaur, and from the last side a magic key."

"You're out of your mind," muttered Scrooey-Looey.

The flamingo took the pebble. He looked at it carefully.

"My dear, you are right. You may travel on your way."

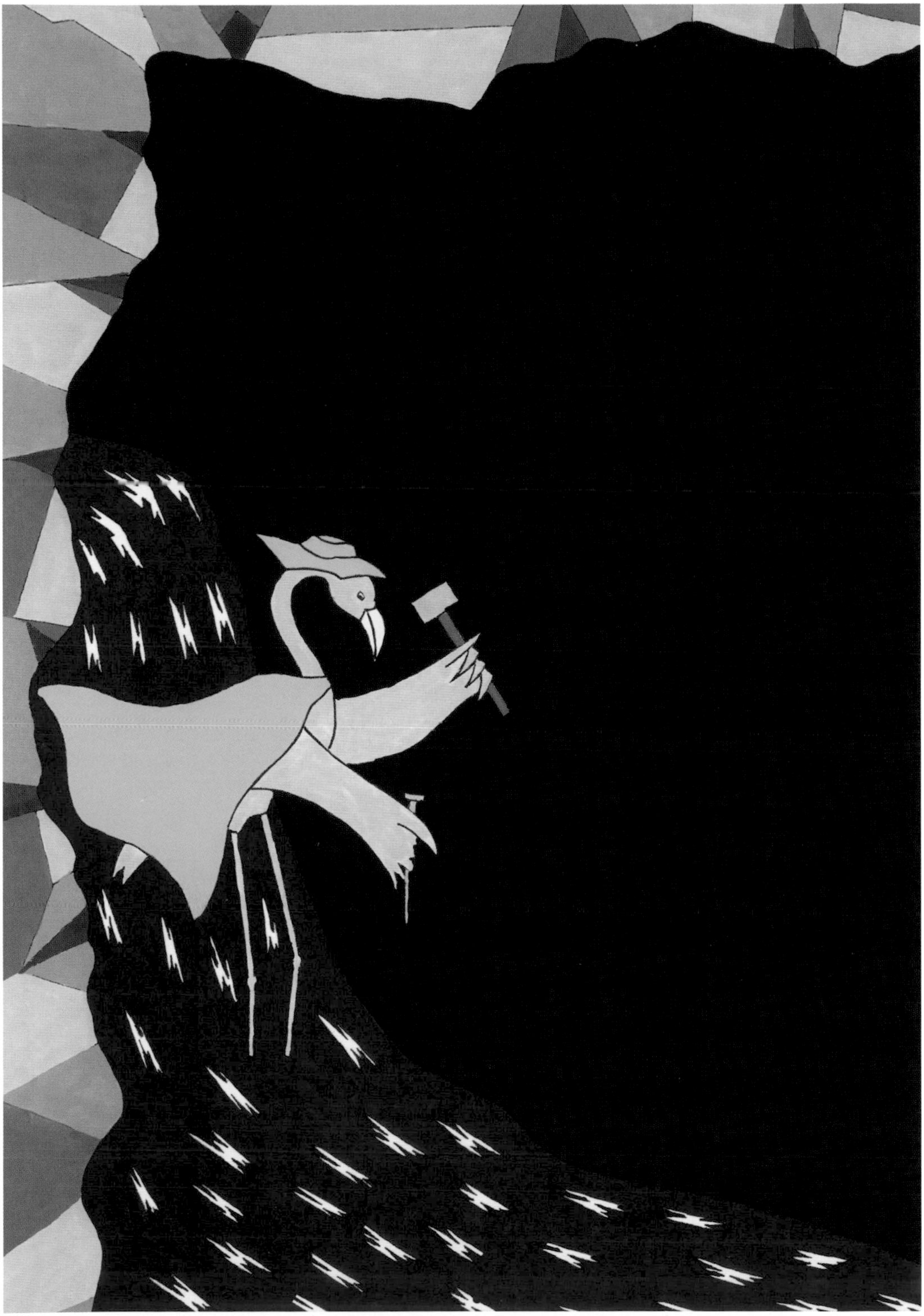

The boys and Scrooey-Looey wandered deeper into the cavern. The walls were no longer carved into fantastic shapes, but contained wide veins of crystal which shone with strange light.

As boys and rabbit walked deeper in, the veins grew wider, the dim gold light grew stronger, filling their bodies with strange warmth, in which they seemed to melt, until they could hardly tell where their bodies ended and the glowing light began.

With the light and warmth came music, rising and falling like waves breaking on a shore, echoing in the cave, first loud, then soft. The music filled the boys with a longing to sing of sun and summer days, of gentle countryside and fields of barley, dry stone wall and hawthorn hedge, dusty earth and white cow parsley. With light, warmth and music, the boys felt a sense of awe: that they were very small and in the presence of a mighty power.

"It's hot," moaned Scrooey-Looey, wiping a paw across his face. "I'll stop here and carve my initials on the wall."

Scrooey-Looey bent down, picked up a piece of crystal and was about to carve his initials on the wall when a great voice boomed, "Stop that rabbit!"

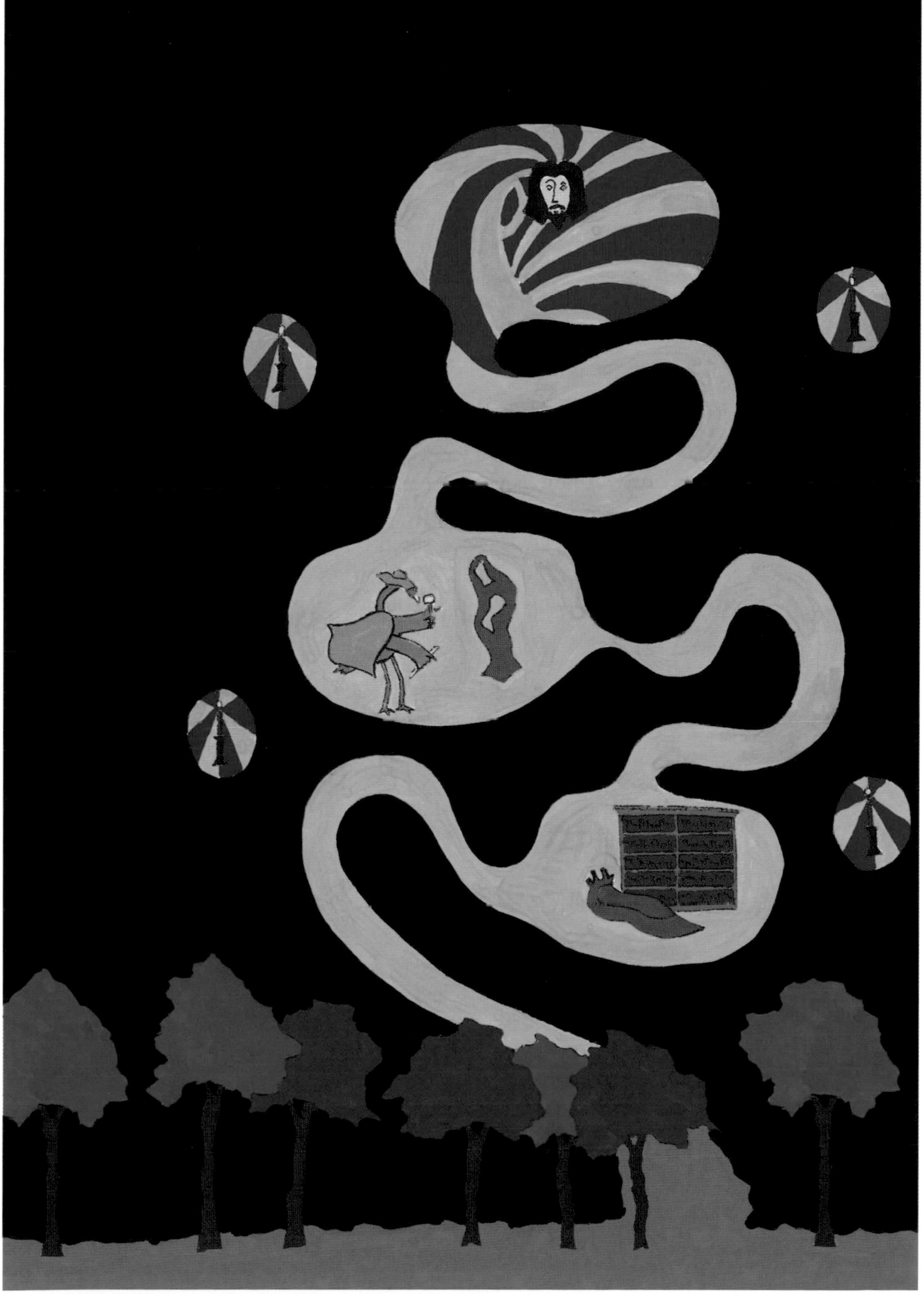

Scrooey-Looey dropped the crystal. His teeth began to chatter, his legs and arms to shake and tremble. In front of them stood a tall figure, around his neck a key of crystal. The boys hardly dared look at the Keeper of the Crystal Key, but Benjamin shuffled forward, took the rabbit by the hand and stammered politely, "Please do not hurt him. He's my friend."

"I do not intend to," said the Keeper, "but he is such a nuisance. Whenever he finds anything of beauty he carves his initials on it. Why have you come to the Crystal Kingdom?"

"To fetch the crystal key."

"To save Snuggle."

"And the Gardener."

"And the Land of Ramion."

The Keeper smiled, and bending low, placed the key around Benjamin's neck. The boys and Scrooey-Looey stretched out hands, and formed a circle, their eyes spellbound by the light which shone from the crystal key. Warmth, light and music danced within them, and closing their eyes their bodies dissolved in light and song, which filled the cavern in praise of the Gardener.

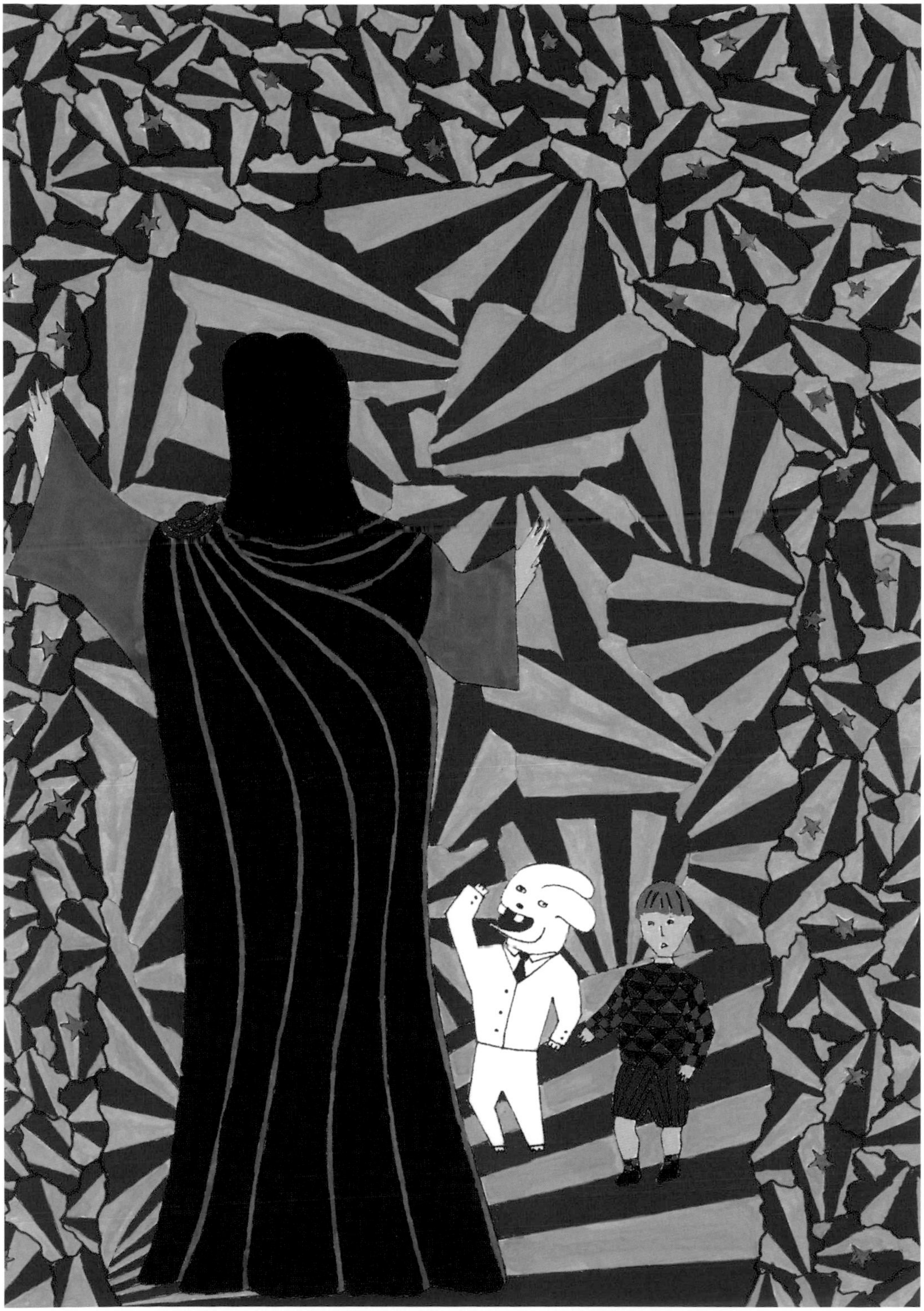

CHAPTER NINE

When the boys and Scrooey-Looey looked around them, they were no longer in the Crystal Kingdom, but in a gully where the two dragons were waiting for them.

"That did not take long," said Eric gravely.

"We hardly had time to brew a cup of tea," added Drago.

The boys and rabbit climbed up on to the dragons, and the dragons flew above the mountains, landing on a barren hillside just above the witches' camp. In the middle was the block of crystal in which Snuggle lay imprisoned.

The witches danced and chanted, volcanoes erupted, filling the air with choking smoke.

"We must wait until it gets dark," said Julius. "Then we shall creep down and free Snuggle."

"You must be joking!" squeaked Scrooey-Looey. "I'll stay here!"

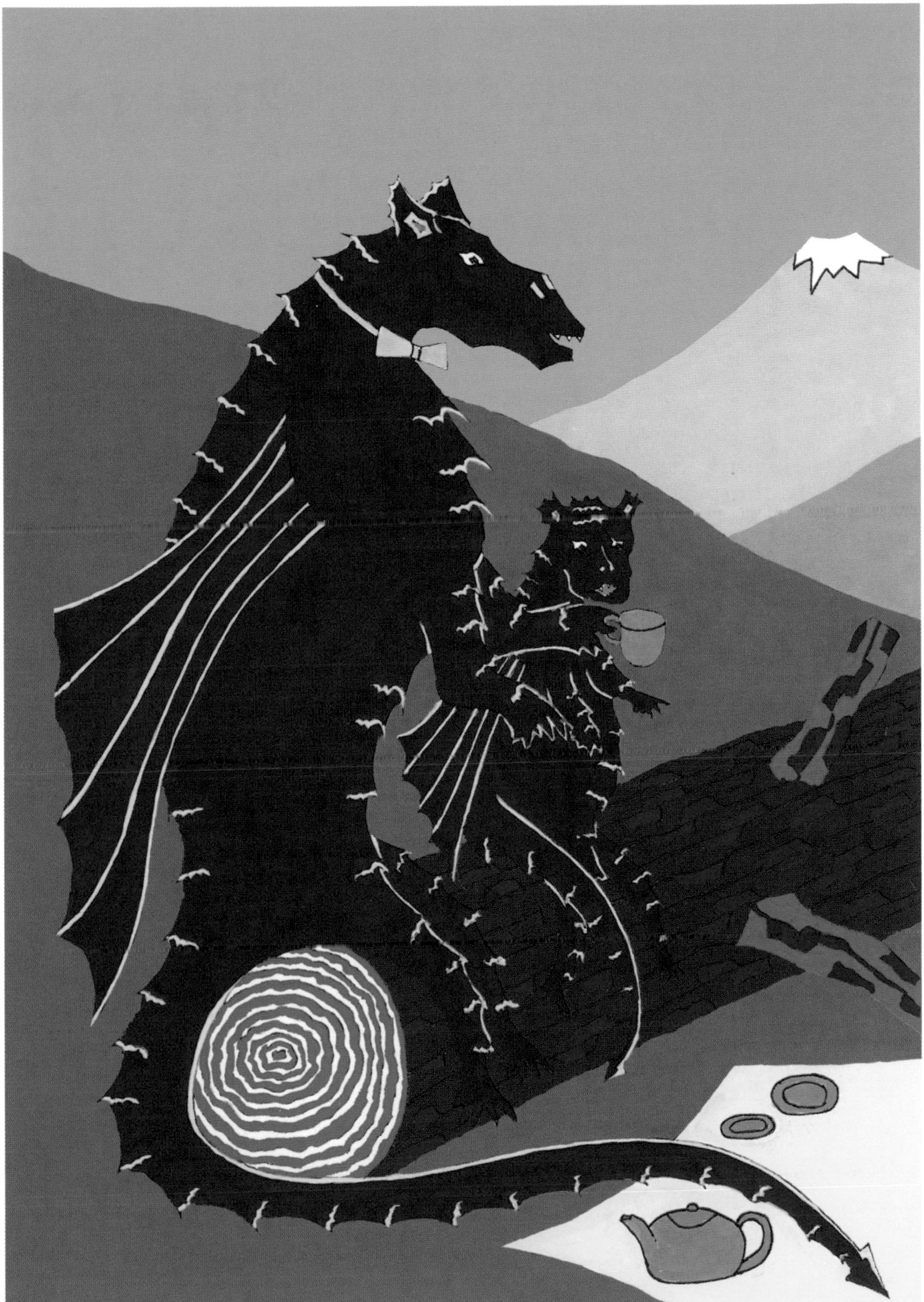

The boys waited until dark, then with the witches fast asleep crept down the mountainside, crouching low, slipping between the rocks, keeping in the shadow.

Birds of prey circled in the sky, monstrous bats brushed their cheeks, as snakes and spiders slithered through their legs. All around volcanoes spat out fire and smoke, blotting out the moon.

The boys reached the circle of witches sleeping around the remains of the fire. Beside the witches was a magic cauldron, in the middle of the circle the block of crystal. The boys crawled between the witches, inched towards the block of crystal. The block was so high they could not reach the top to fit the key in the slot.

"Link shoulders Alexander," whispered Julius. Julius and Alex placed arms around each other's shoulders and braced themselves against the block of crystal. "Now Benje. Up you go."

Benjamin scrambled up his brothers' backs and onto their shoulders, took the key off his neck, and as his brothers swayed and groaned under his weight, was about to stretch up and fit the key in the slot, when Griselda stirred, opened one eye, and murmured with delight, "My supper! Julius! Alexander! Benjamin! Come to Griselda!"

The boys gasped in horror, but with a strength beyond their own, stood firm, did not run, as Griselda rose to get them.

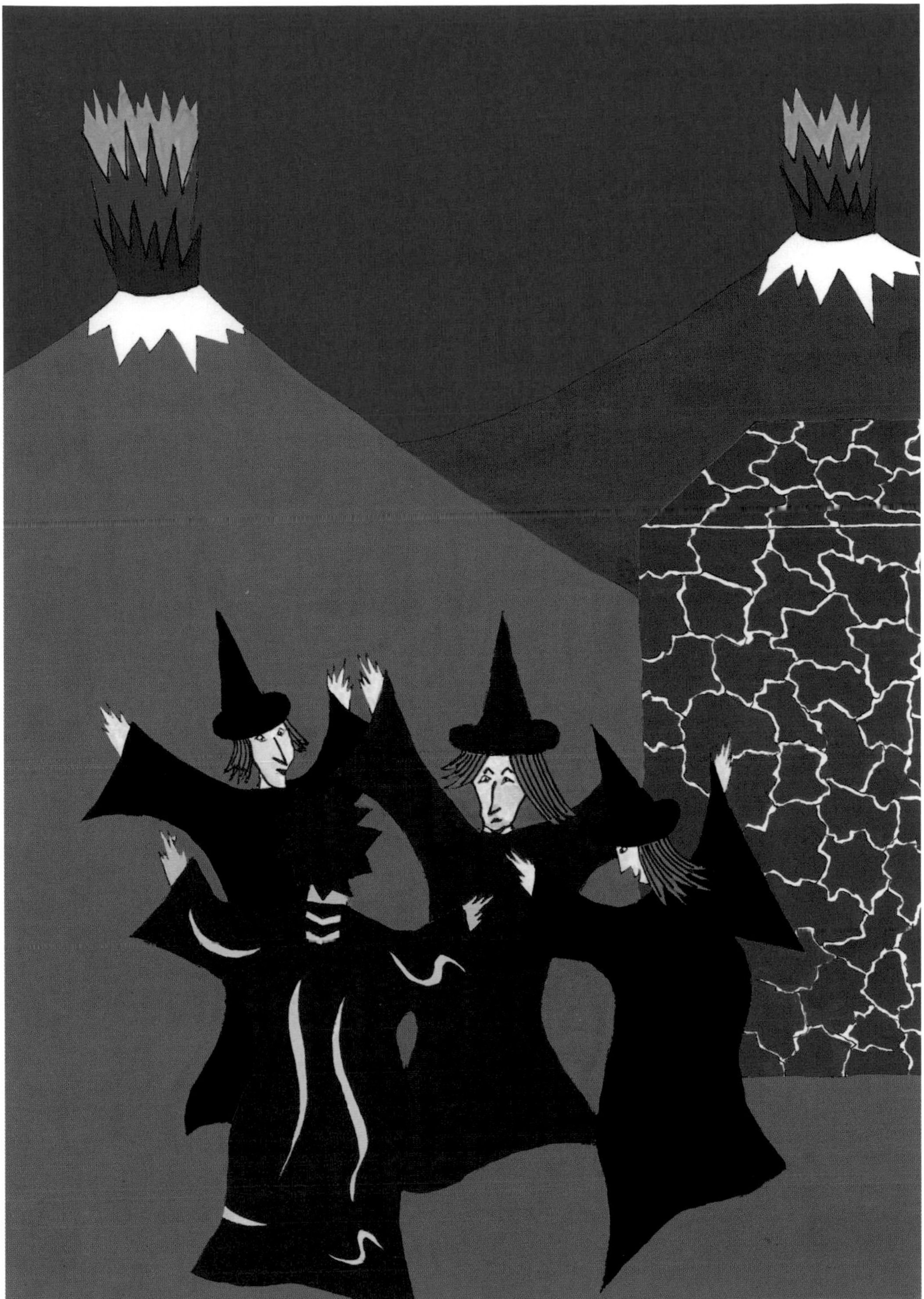

Before Griselda could grab the boys, the flap of dragons' wings filled the air. Scrooey-Looey, waving a stick on Drago's back, had grown strangely brave, squeaking excitedly, "Attack! Attack!"

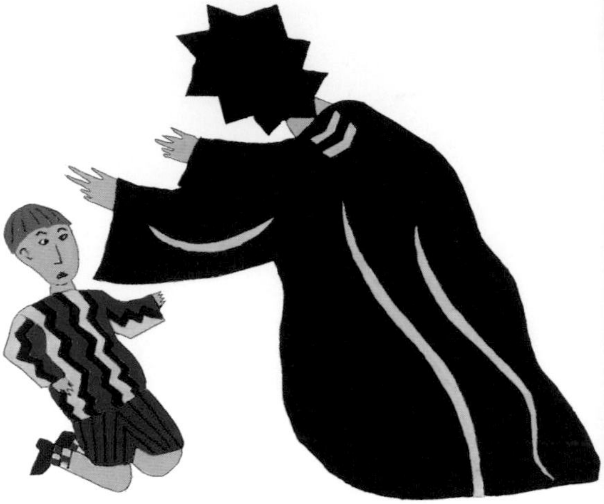

Drago spat from long range.

The ball of fire landed in the magic cauldron. It exploded in evil confusion, filling the air with sprites and ghouls, which danced amongst the witches and crawled in their hair. All the witches (except Griselda) screamed and fled, but when the sprites and ghouls saw the crystal key clasped in Benjamin's hand, they melted away.

Benjamin stretched up and fitted the key in the crystal block. There was a sharp crack as the crystal split in two. From his prison, weak and trembling, Snuggle struggled to his feet. He looked at the boys, who had fallen to the ground in a heap.

Screaming "My supper! My supper!" Griselda reached forward, caught Julius by the neck, scratched him with a ring filled with poison. Then she turned to Alexander.

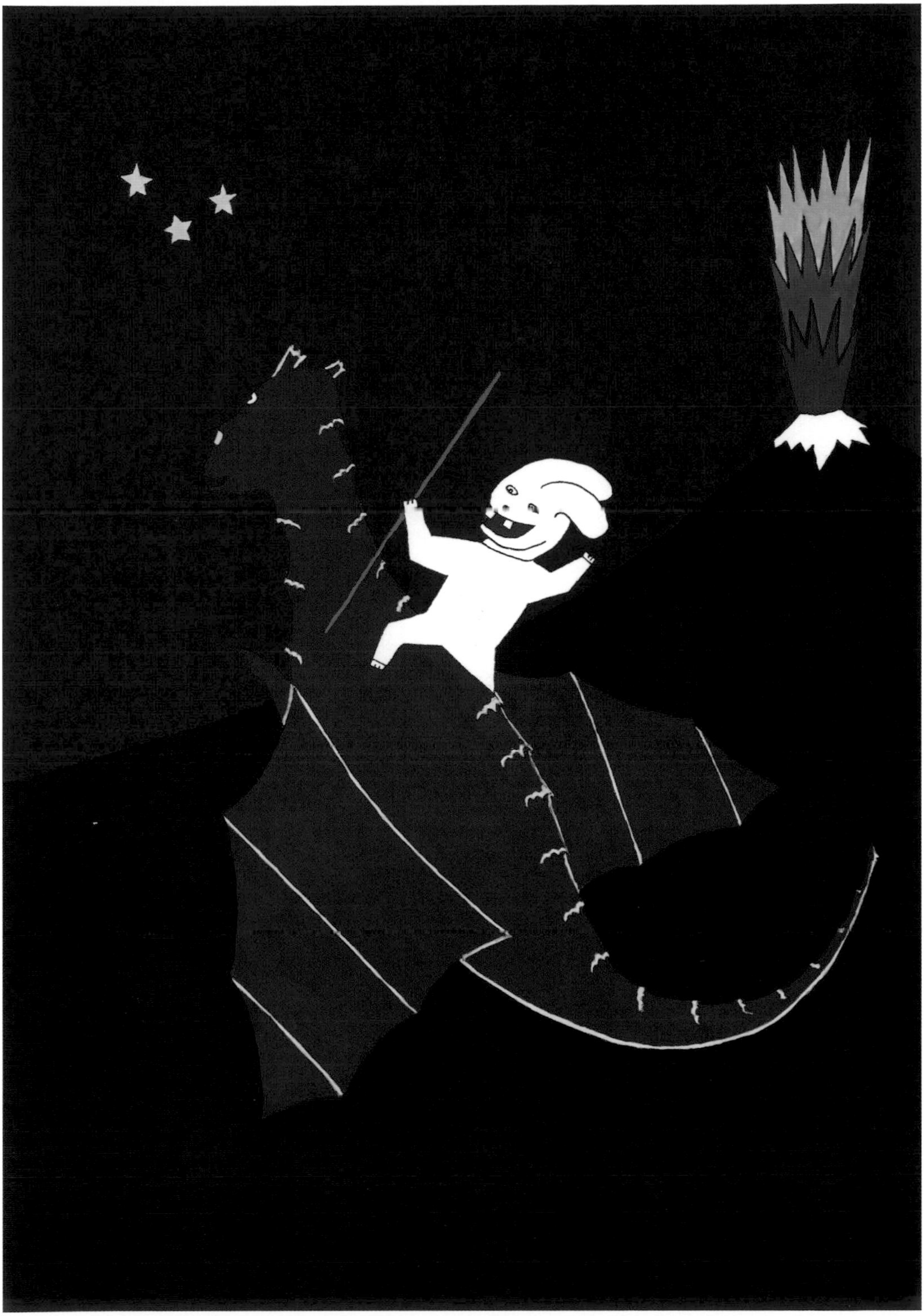

Snuggle summoned what remained of his strength. He leapt on to Griselda, sinking teeth and claws into her horrid nose.

At that moment Eric landed. Alexander and Benjamin lifted Julius on to the dragon's back. He lay senseless, face pale, pulse faint, hardly breathing. His brothers jumped up beside him, tears in their eyes, rubbing his hands and cheeks – but he did not stir.

Snuggle gave Griselda one last bite (she screamed loudly) and with a great leap joined the boys on Eric's back. As Eric sailed into the sky, Drago flew to him, spitting flame (just for the fun of it).

Very soon the dragons were landing on the hillside above the Garden. The Guide was there to greet them.

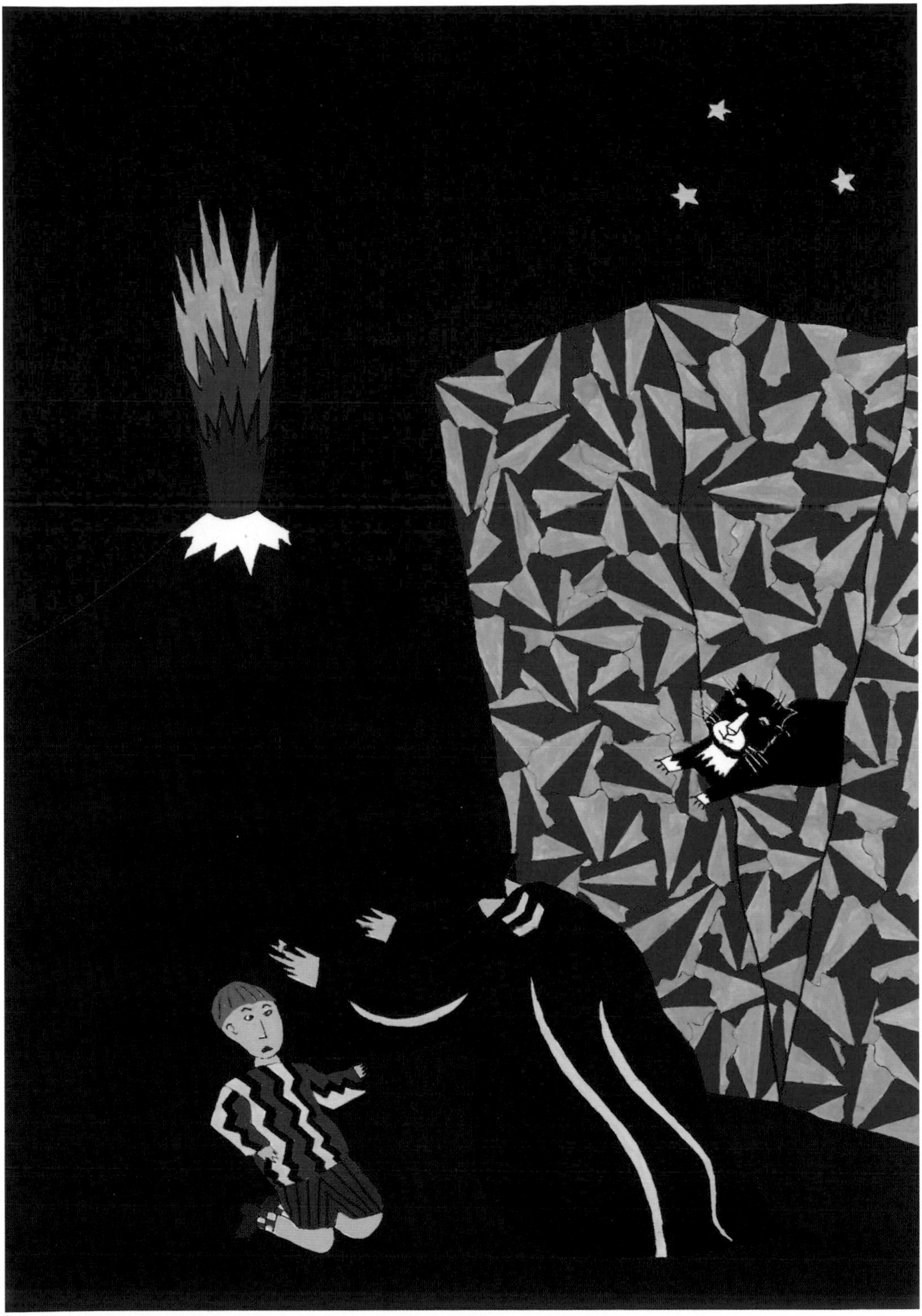

Led by the Guide Alexander, Benjamin, Snuggle and Scrooey-Looey carried Julius's lifeless body down the gully to the Garden. The door was open.

Death had departed from the Garden. Grass, plants and trees had sprung to life, and it was high summer: roses were in full colour, birds singing, butterflies and bees flying from flower to flower.

The Gardener strode towards them, and they followed him between scented shrubs and trees, until deep within the Garden, they found a secret place, where a rose arching overhead filled the air with heavy perfume. There they laid Julius down on a bench.

The rose began to fade, slowly to wither, and as it did, colour returned to the boy's cheeks. He stirred, sighed, suddenly sat up and looked about him.

"The rose is dead. It's dead!" Julius cried.

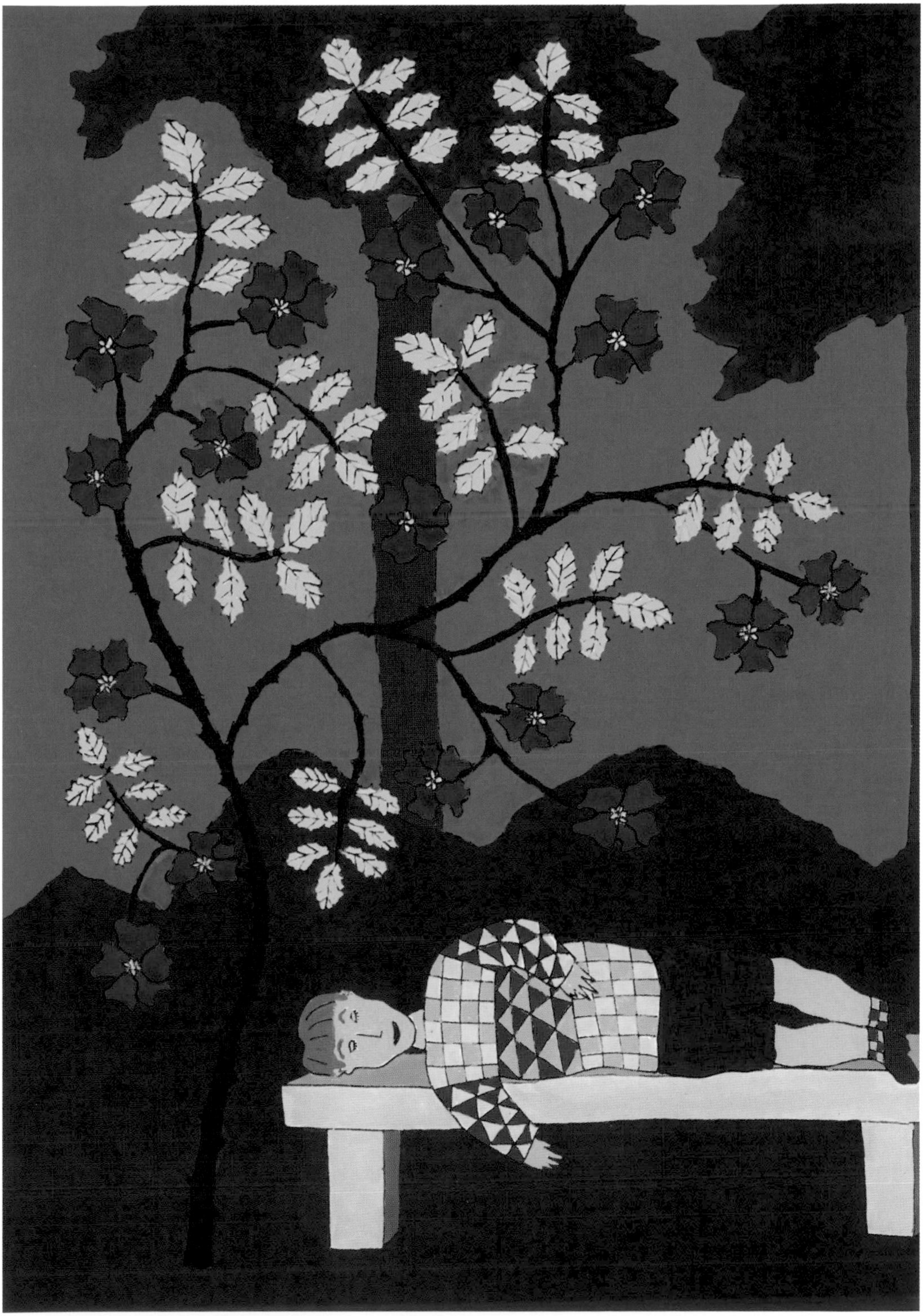

The Gardener took Julius by the hand and he saw the Garden restored to life, except the secret place where the rose had died.

"Why did the rose die?" Julius asked the Gardener.

"Its beauty took the poison from your body – in giving life it died. But I took two cuttings. I shall plant one and soon the secret place will be as beautiful as it was before. The other cutting is for you. Put it in your pocket and plant it in your father's garden. If ever you are tempted to despair, look at its beauty, and think of the rose, which took the poison from your body, and in giving life did die."

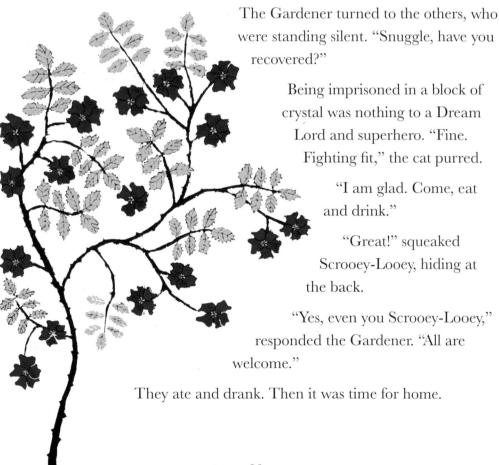

The Gardener turned to the others, who were standing silent. "Snuggle, have you recovered?"

Being imprisoned in a block of crystal was nothing to a Dream Lord and superhero. "Fine. Fighting fit," the cat purred.

"I am glad. Come, eat and drink."

"Great!" squeaked Scrooey-Looey, hiding at the back.

"Yes, even you Scrooey-Looey," responded the Gardener. "All are welcome."

They ate and drank. Then it was time for home.

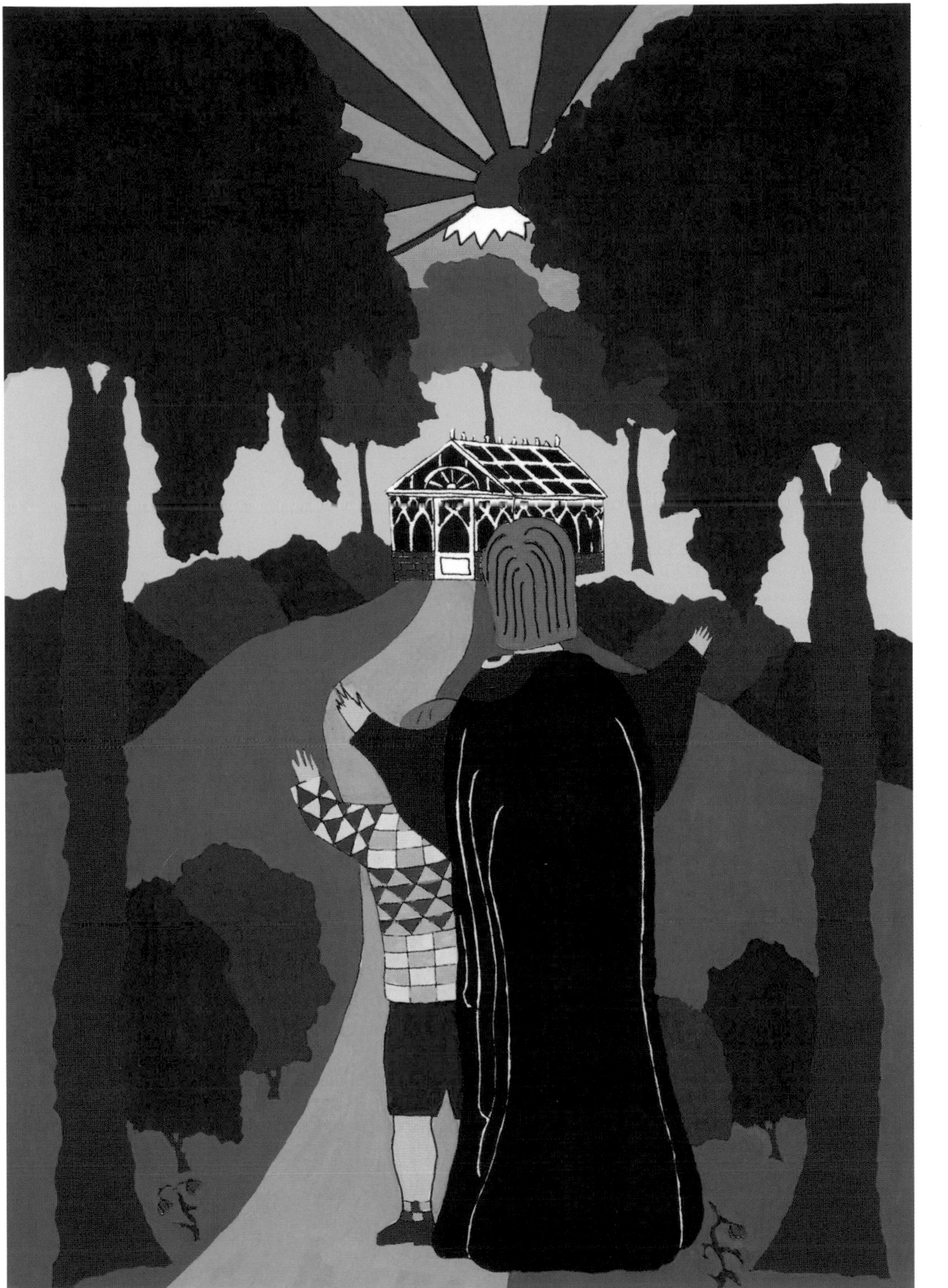

Available Now:

TALES OF RAMION
THE LAND OF LOST HAIR
Frank Hinks

The Land of Lost Hair No. 1

The witch Griselda casts a spell to make the boys travel to her, but the slime of maggot is past its sell-by date and the boys and their parents only lose their hair. Snuggle (Dream Lord and superhero) takes the boys to the Land of Lost Hair, but Griselda follows, and sends giant combs, scissors and hair driers to get the boys. "Boy kebabs for tea!" cried Griselda jubilantly.

ISBN: 9781909938113

TALES OF RAMION
THE VICAR'S CHICKENS
Frank Hinks

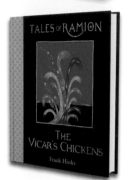

The Vicar's Chickens No. 2

Snuggle's weakness for the Vicar's chickens drives the Vicar mad. But when the witch Griselda sends fireballs on the garden of The Old Vicarage, Snuggle (by mistake) magics not only the boys but the church and Vicar to the Land of Ramion. The Vicar becomes a child again, learns not to fear a thing, and dancing up to the witch calls her "Auntie Griselda" and (whilst she is in a state of shock) takes her magic staff with surprising consequences.

ISBN: 9781909938175

TALES OF RAMION
CREATURES OF THE FOREST
Frank Hinks

Creatures of the Forest No. 4

In the magical forest there are Globerous Ghosts, Venomous Vampires, Scary Scots and Mystic Mummies, who (like other mummies) cannot stand boys who pick their noses. The boys are in constant danger of being turned into ghostly globs, piles of dust or being exploded by very loud bagpipe music. Thankfully, Ducky Rocky, Racing Racoons and the Hero Hedgehogs are there to help.

ISBN: 9781909938151

TALES OF RAMION
THE BODY COLLECTOR
Frank Hinks

The Body Collector No. 15

Charlie Stench the Body Collector collects bodies: the heads he turns into floating skulls. When the witch Griselda consorts with five mini-skulls (so evil that they want to eat her and her guards the dim daft dwarves) Boris the skull is only prepared to rescue her if she promises to get him back his body. But Griselda keeps her fingers crossed so the promise will not count. When Griselda and Boris visit the Body Collector nothing works out as they expect.

ISBN: 9781909938212

TALES OF RAMION
BORIS AND THE DUMB SKULLS
Frank Hinks

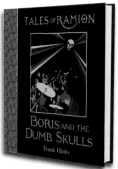

BORIS AND THE DUMB SKULLS No. 16

Fed up of being bullied by the witch Griselda Boris the skull and the dim daft dwarves decide to form a punk rock band and seek fame and fortune. But just before they leave for their first gig two of Griselda's dead ancestors break out of their glass tanks beneath the ruined tower. Fifi Vicomtesse de Grunch is very keen on dancing. Her husband the Vicomte expresses his feelings towards Fifi's dancing partners with a spanner. Not surprisingly the boys' father comes to regret dancing with her.

ISBN: 9781909938199

TALES OF RAMION
THE DREAM THIEF
Frank Hinks

THE DREAM THIEF No. 17

When the Dream Thief steals their mother's dream of being an artist the boys and their Dream Lord cat, Snuggle, set off to rescue her dream. The party, including their mother as a six-year-old child, passes through the Place of Nightmares (where butterflies with butterfly nets, game birds with shotguns and fish with fishing rods try to get them) and enter the Land of Dreams where with the help of Little Dream and the Hero Dreamhogs they seek the stronghold of the Dream Thief and brave the mighty Gnargs, warrior servants of the Princess of the Night.

ISBN: 9781909938076

TALES OF RAMION
FRANKIE AND THE DANCING FURIES
Frank Hinks

FRANKIE AND THE DANCING FURIES No. 18

A storm summoned by the witch Griselda (unwitting tool of the Princess of the Night) attacks The Old Vicarage and carries off the boys' father along with Griselda, the skull Boris (whom the Princess wants for her living art collection), the dwarves and the boys' mother as a child. The father's love of rock and roll distorts the spell and all travel to the land of the Dancing Furies where the spirit of the great rock god Jimi (Hendrix) takes possession of the father's body. When he causes flowers to grow in the hair of the Dancing Furies they reveal their true nature as Goddesses of Vengeance.

ISBN: 9781909938090

TALES OF RAMION

You can explore the magical world of Ramion by visiting the website

www.ramion-books.com

Share Ramion Moments on Facebook

TALES OF RAMION
FACT AND FANTASY

O nce upon a time not so long ago there lived in The Old Vicarage, Shoreham, Kent
(a village south of London) three boys (Julius, Alexander and Benjamin) with their
mother, father and Snuggle, the misnamed family cat who savaged dogs and had a weakness for
the vicar's chickens. At birthdays there were magic shows with Scrooey-Looey, a glove puppet
with great red mouth who was always rude.

The boys with Snuggle

J ulius was a demanding child. Each night he wanted a different story. But he would help his father.
"Dad tonight I want a story about the witch Griselda" (who had purple hair like his artist
mother) "and the rabbit Scrooey-Looey and it starts like this…" His father then had to take
over the story not knowing where it was going (save that the witch was not allowed to eat the
children). Out of such stories grew the Tales of Ramion which were enacted with the boys'
mother as Griselda and the boys' friends as Griselda's guards, the Dim Daft Dwarves (a role
which came naturally to children).

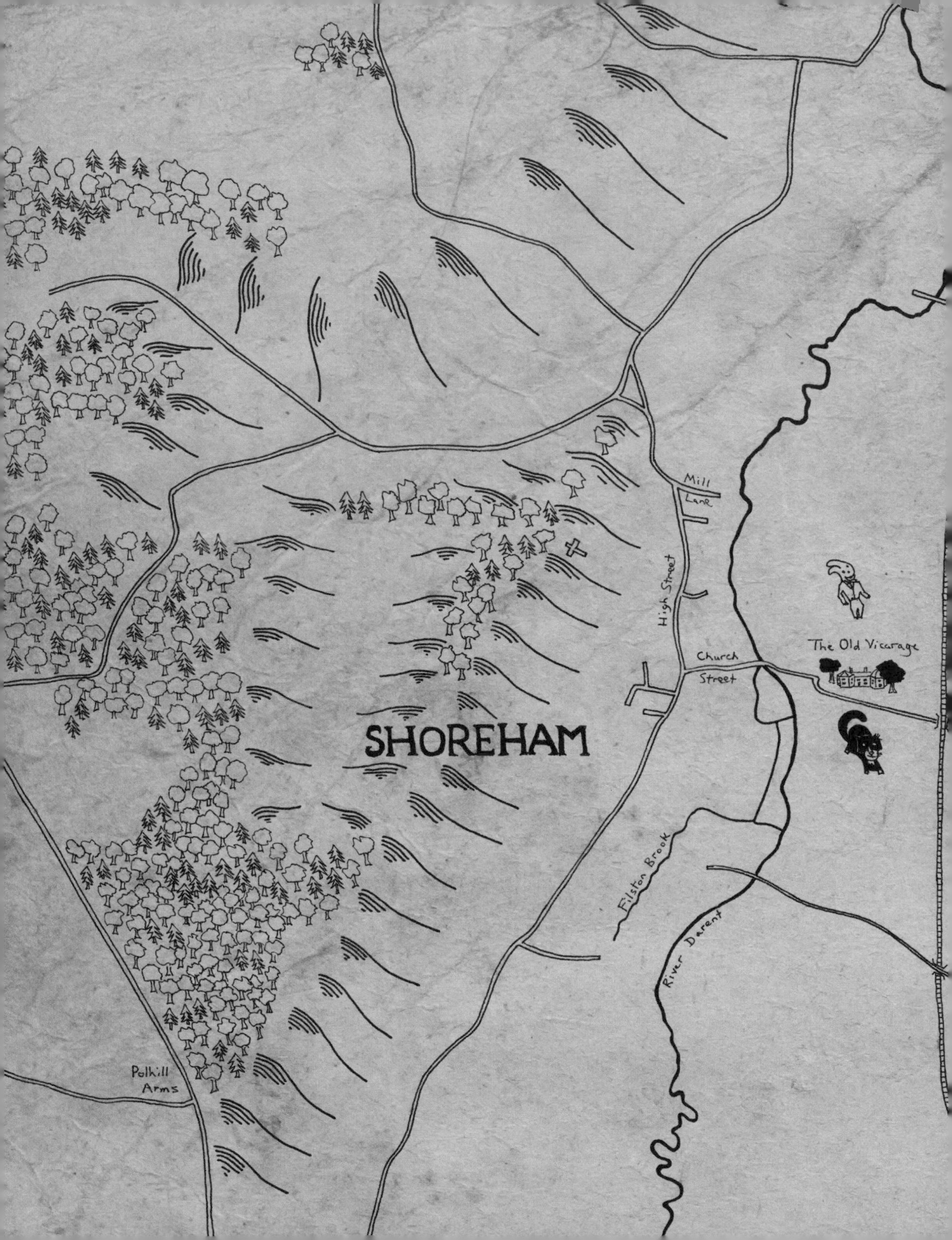
SHOREHAM
Mill Lane
High Street
Church Street
The Old Vicarage
Filston Brook
River Darent
Polhill Arms